DEVIL'S ELBOW

(A HARBOR SECRET - BOOK 2)

This ebook is a work of fiction. The names, characters, places, and incidents are products of the writer's imagination or have been used fictitiously and are not to be construed as real. Any resemblance to persons, living or dead, actual events, locales, or organizations is entirely coincidental.

Edited by Cassandra Heos

Cover design by Sheri McGathy

Author photo by Maya Murshak Parks

Cover photos (front and back) by Maya Murshak Parks

Special thanks to Historians Eric Hemenway & Richard Wiles

Thanks to Thom & Janet Blanck and Robert & Jane Cardinal

Thanks to the Michigan History Center

To the people of Northern Michigan who have been

so supportive.

Devil's Elbow

Prologue

The screams of the girls penetrated the thin tent, drifted into the field surrounding it, and were finally absorbed by the edges of the thick forest.

"Keep it down in here," Judy advised as she stuck her head into the tent. "We troop leaders are trying to enjoy a bottle of sparkling cider in peace."

"Sorry, Aunt Judy," Kylie apologized, throwing her aunt a nine-year-old grin of uneven teeth, "but Vicky just had a really scary ghost story."

Judy sniffed in dismissal. "There are no such things as ghosts."

"Yes, there are," Cammy corrected.

Judy looked at the nine-year-old with wavy blonde hair and freckles. "No, there aren't."

Cammy leaned in to the lantern that sat in the middle of the circle of Girl Scouts. "Yes, there are, and I'll prove it."

"How?" Judy asked impatiently.

"By telling a true story."

Judy started to roll her eyes.

Kylie scooted over. "Come sit next to me, Aunt Judy."

Judy hesitated. "I really should be getting back. I don't want Stella to eat all the cheese."

"Staaaaaay," the girls pleaded in unison as Kylie pulled at her aunt's arm.

Judy let out a sigh and dropped to the floor of the tent, crossing her legs. "Okay, fine. Tell your true ghost story."

Kylie wrapped her arm around her aunt's and snuggled into it as Cammy started to speak.

"This all started when my mom was a baby," Cammy began as she leaned her face closer to the lantern for emphasis. "My grandma and her baby were driving home to Cross Village through a terrible snow storm when they saw a man walking beside the road."

"Did he jump in front of the car?" Jennifer asked.

"Shhh," the other girls quieted the interruption.

Cammy waited for the silence to return before continuing. "He was tall and thin, wearing a tan coat that went to his knees, and carrying a satchel."

"What's a satchel?" Kylie interrupted.

"It's like a briefcase but made of soft leather," Cammy informed.

"Oh."

Judy smiled fondly at the girls as Cammy continued.

"He had long, scraggly black hair, and his face was very pale." Her own face was calm as she stared into the light from the lantern and continued. "My mom was just a baby and sleeping in the back seat, but her mother stopped to offer the man a ride."

"Then he stabbed them all?" Laura interrupted.

"Uh, no. Cammy wouldn't be alive if that happened," Jennifer pointed out.

"Duh," Kylie chimed in. Judy nudged her, and Kylie held back further comment.

"So then what happened?" Laura asked, pushing a strand of

long, blonde hair behind an ear.

"So he got into the car, but he never said a word," Cammy continued. "My grandma tried to make conversation, but he just stared straight ahead and didn't comment."

"So then what happened?" Kylie couldn't help herself.

Cammy leaned back and parted her hands mystically. "So, when they got to Devil's Elbow, he started to bang on the car door. My grandma stopped the car, and he got out without ever saying a word."

"So where does the ghost part come in?" Judy asked impatiently. "Seriously, there was only one block of cheese left, and Stella needs more cheese like she needs a hole in the head."

Kylie gave a yank on her arm, and Judy bit her lip.

"When the man got out of the car and my grandma started to pull away, she looked in the rearview mirror, and he was gone."

"Well, they were in the middle of a snow storm," Judy commented.

"No. My grandma stopped the car and looked back, and he

had totally disappeared." Cammy made a gesture with her hands to replicate the disappearance.

"Okay. So is that the end of the story?" Judy asked, starting to rise.

"No," Cammy continued. "Three days later, my grandma was working in her kitchen in Cross Village. She turned around and saw him looking in the window at her."

"Eek!" the girls shrieked.

"Wait," Cammy continued. "When my grandma went outside, he wasn't there. When she looked under the window he had been peering into, there were no footprints in the snow."

"Eek!" the girls shrieked again.

"Yeah," Judy commented as she slowly got to her feet, "I think this might have happened during your grandma's cocktail hour, which I happen to be missing." She stepped to the door and turned back. "Try to keep it down, girls. I don't want anyone calling out Harbor Vice with noise complaints."

CHAPTER 1

Kylie watched her dog Cupcake tiptoe next to the edges of the waves as they rushed into the Good Hart Beach.

"I don't think she's ever going to learn to swim," she told local fire chief and boyfriend Jason Lange, who stood thigh deep in the cold water of Lake Michigan.

"Try throwing a stick out," he suggested.

Kylie glanced around the white sand beach before picking up a stick, waving it at Cupcake, and throwing it a short distance towards Jason. "Go get it, Cupcake."

Cupcake yipped but made no effort to get more than the bottoms of her paws wet. She skipped around anxiously.

Jason waded closer to shore and picked up the stick. "Cupcake, look," he said as he waved it in the air before dropping it in the water in front of him. "Look, Cupcake," he tried again when she didn't respond.

The black, six-month-old puppy wasn't looking at the fire chief. She was looking behind her towards the tall beach grass that separated the beach from the woods.

"Oh, no," Kylie heard Jason say as she started to follow Cupcake's gaze.

At the edge of the grass was a young deer trying to get to the lake for a drink.

Kylie made a lunge for Cupcake, but it was too late. Cupcake darted towards the deer, and the deer darted down the beach.

"Cupcake!" Kylie called before taking off down the beach after the puppy. Kylie was a seasoned runner, but the puppy was faster, and the deer was fastest. She hadn't made it fifty yards before Jason passed her, his long, strong strides quickly leaving her behind.

The deer ran down the beach before turning left and running through the grass and into the forest. Cupcake and Jason followed. Kylie took up the rear.

"Ouch! Ooch! Ouch!" she exclaimed as her bare feet encountered the prickly gravel road of Lower Shore Drive. She hopped painfully across the road and followed the deer path towards the bottom of the bluff. "Cupcake!" she called as she headed into dense forest.

"She's over here," Jason called.

Kylie stepped over sticks as she trotted up the deer path that ended at a small pond hidden in a narrow ravine. Cupcake stood at the edge of the pond, her hair on end as she growled towards a thicket of saplings.

"The deer went in there," Jason gestured towards the small thicket.

"Well, grab Cupcake so she doesn't scare the poor thing."

"She's pretty worked up. You grab her."

Kylie let out a sigh and stepped towards the puppy, who let out an uncharacteristically loud growl. "Cupcake Marie, what is the matter with you?" Kylie scolded.

"Marie?" Jason lifted an eyebrow at her. "She has a middle name now?"

Kylie ignored him as she stepped towards the growling puppy. "What's the matter, Cuppie?"

Cupcake kept her focus on the thicket. Kylie grabbed the dog's collar and held her back before dropping to her knees to peer ahead and see what the puppy saw. "Oh, my gosh!"

"What?" Jason moved next to her and dropped to all fours to peer into the thicket.

"It's an opening in the bluff."

Jason looked at the small deer trembling inside the opening that was barely large enough to house it.

"You'd never notice it if you weren't down at this level," Kylie whispered.

"Let's move back and let it leave," Jason advised, starting to crawl backwards.

"Come on, Cupcakie," Kylie said as she lifted the forty-five-pound puppy into her arms and moved towards the road.

Cupcake barked and tried to break free, completely unhappy with the situation.

"Let's go back and get the truck," Jason decided. "Maybe the deer will feel comfortable enough to leave without us around."

Kylie struggled to hang on to the puppy that squirmed and fought the whole way back to the truck. "I've never seen you like this," Kylie told the large puppy. "What is wrong with you?"

"Maybe she likes venison," Jason commented dryly.

Kylie threw him a disapproving look. "She doesn't even chase squirrels. That deer was bigger than she was. It's just not like her."

A half hour later, the truck pulled up to the deer path, and the couple walked up the trail, Cupcake lagging behind in a reluctant walk on her leash.

Kylie looked at the thick and silent trees that lined either side of the path and felt herself shiver. For the first time she noticed how quiet it was. "Where are we, anyway?"

Jason's eyes traveled up the bluff that towered above them and observed how it sunk in sharply to hide the pond. "Devil's Elbow."

"Her hair is standing up again," Kylie observed Cupcake when they reached the pond. "This is so weird."

Jason dropped to all fours and crawled towards the cavern. "The deer is gone. Come on."

Cupcake growled again.

"Come on, Cuppie, the mean ol' deer is gone," Kylie assured.

The couple crawled forward through the thicket on their hands and knees, dragging a growling Cupcake behind them.

Jason pulled his cell phone out of his pocket, switched on the built-in flashlight, and shined it into the small opening. "It must have been carved out by that spring coming out of the base of the bluff," he observed as his light reflected off of the trickle of water running down the back wall and through the center of the cave.

"And it looks like the place where baby deer go to die," Kylie observed.

Jason moved his flashlight to illuminate the array of tiny hooves and bits of bone in the center of the cavern. His expression sobered, and his tone lowered. "Stay here."

Kylie watched as he crawled into the small cave for a closer look before coming out.

"Let's go."

"What did you see?"

He crawled back through the underbrush. "Let's go," he repeated.

Cupcake was more than happy to oblige as she pulled Kylie along after Jason.

Back in his truck, Jason rested his hands on the steering wheel and stared straight ahead.

"What is it? What did you see?" Kylie asked.

Without turning his head, Jason answered, "I think those were human remains." Shocked, Kylie didn't respond; and he continued, "I'm going to have to call it in."

CHAPTER 2

"Muckwa, you're so silly!" Little Fawn called to her large, brown dog as he frolicked ahead of her in the ravine, turning to stick his butt in the air as he struck a playful pose with a stick in his mouth.

Her moccasins padded softly on the earth as she ran up the deer trail after him. "Come, Muckwa. Bring me the stick."

Muckwa frolicked ahead and turned back to look at her.

"Do you want me to chase you?"

Muckwa struck his playful pose again.

"Okay," she giggled, "here I come!"

Little Fawn lunged forward, just missing the stick in Muckwa's mouth and causing her long, black hair to fall over her face. Without a thought, she threw it back as she straightened. "Oh, you're fast, but not fast enough!" She ran up the ravine next to the small stream, following the dog with the stick. She was giggling and chasing Muckwa when she saw him stop and look at something just ahead.

Abruptly stopping, her gaze followed Muckwa's as she heard him issue a long, low warning growl.

Her heart stopped for a moment as she saw the tall warrior ahead of her. He was intimidating with his heavily-tattooed, lean, muscular arms and legs. His head was shaved with nothing left but a thick tuft of a black ponytail at the top.

She saw he wore nothing but a loin cloth and moccasins as her eyes moved up his body, feeling tiny tingles of sensation through her own body as her eyes unabashedly studied him. His hard eyes visibly softened when hers reached his and he realized she wasn't a threat.

Recognizing him as a fellow Odawa, she smiled softly and lifted a hand to him in greeting.

A smile flickered at the corners of his mouth but was quickly extinguished before it fully formed.

"Who are you?" he asked.

"Wa-wash-ay-wesh Koons," she answered quietly.

He nodded. "Are you Odawa, Little Fawn?"

She nodded, slightly intimidated by this serious man.

He made no effort to move towards her. "Why have I not seen you before?"

"My family lives on Manitoulin Island. This is our first time in the summer camp."

He nodded his acknowledgment again. "Why did you leave the island?"

Little Fawn stepped forward, hoping to speak from a more comfortable distance. "My grandmother spent summers at the camp when she was a girl. She wanted to return. My brother, Ojig, and I came with her."

He nodded again, not making an effort to move to a more comfortable distance but watching her carefully.

"Do you go to the island in the winter?" she asked, taking another step closer.

He shook his head. "No. I go south along the lake."

Little Fawn nodded, adding another step and closing the gap between them with a casual stealth. A long moment passed as they sized each other up.

"You should not be out here alone," he warned her. "It is closer to the Muscodesh village than the Odawa camp."

She nodded and smiled again. "Thank you. I will remember that." She looked around and gestured. "It is just such a lovely ravine with the small creek running through it, we could not resist following it." She glanced down at her dog, who was watching the warrior carefully.

He nodded solemnly again and tilted his head towards Muckwa. "It is good you brought your dog with you, but you should not stray this far from the camp alone again."

She leaned and ran her fingers through Muckwa's thick brown fur. "I have not met other friends yet, so Muckwa is my companion for now. He goes everywhere I go."

The man didn't respond, and Little Fawn looked with a calm interest at the heavily-tattooed man who would intimidate others. "You are a warrior?"

"Yes."

She nodded, realizing the violence that that entailed, and her eyes drifted to his feet and the ground around them as her mind searched for something else to say.

"What is your place?" he asked.

Proud of her place in the tribe, she lifted her head and held her chin high. "I am a jingle dress dancer."

"You have been chosen?"

"Yes."

"Have you danced before?"

"Yes, but not in a full dress. My next dance will be full."

He looked at her thoughtfully for a while, still holding his body up rigidly. "I am also a hunter." He lifted his fist to his chest. "I am a very good hunter."

She didn't respond.

"I will bring you pieces for your dress."

Little Fawn nodded and smiled warmly at him. "Thank you."

He lingered, his body feeling a draw to this younger woman.

"My brother and I share my grandmother's wigwam," she

offered weakly. The conversation had become strained, but neither wanted to leave.

"I will watch for you."

Little Fawn fought the urge to lift her hand to touch the beautifully-tattooed body before her and could think of nothing more to do but smile.

"I must go." He took a step back without turning. "I will watch for you," he repeated.

Little Fawn felt a frantic wave rush over her when she realized he was departing. "Wait," she called, not wanting him to leave.

He paused.

Little Fawn's mind spun as she struggled to think of something to say. A soft smile crossing her lips, she asked, "What is your name?"

The smile flickered at the corners of his mouth again but was extinguished before it could form. "Onadesh. I am called Onadesh."

Little Fawn's bright white teeth shown as she looked down to Muckwa. "Muckwa, this is Moon Wanderer."

Muckwa looked up to her and let out a questioning, high-pitched groan.

As Little Fawn's focus turned back to Onadesh, her expression changed to one of surprise. Her eyes scanning the forest around her, she realized that he had disappeared as quickly as he had appeared.

CHAPTER 3

Days passed, and Little Fawn watched for Onadesh with vigilance, constantly scanning the bodies moving busily around the large summer camp.

Her grandmother narrowed her eyes in suspicion as she watched her granddaughter. "Wa-wash-ay-wesh Koons, who do you watch for?"

Blushing, Little Fawn fumbled her words. "Uh, no one, Grandmother," she responded in an unconvincing tone. "There are just so many new faces here, I must try to remember all of them."

Her eyes still narrowed at her granddaughter, she nodded. "But there is one you look for."

Her blush deepening, Little Fawn lowered her head. "Yes, Grandmother. I am sorry I lied."

"Sit and tell me," the old woman gestured to the blanket of colorful patterns spread on the ground outside of their wigwam.

Still avoiding eye contact, Little Fawn sat down and crossed her legs, Muckwa dropping down heavily beside her and letting out a sigh.

"Who is he?"

Picking up a small twig and breaking it between her fingers, she said, "His name is Onadesh."

"Moon Wanderer," she muttered to herself. "What an odd name." She spoke up as she addressed her granddaughter. "He is Odawa?"

Little Fawn nodded, still focused on the twig.

"What is his place?"

"He is a warrior."

The old woman nodded. "Why have I not met this warrior?"

Understanding her assumption, Little Fawn shifted her focus quickly from the twig to her grandmother's brown eyes. "No, Grandmother, it is not like that. I have only met him once when Muckwa and I were playing near a spring."

"He has not asked anything of you?"

"No," she replied in a tone that let her grandmother know she spoke the truth. "I know nothing – "

She was interrupted by two moccasined feet that appeared in front of her. The eyes of the two women moved upward over strong calves and thighs, a loin cloth, and a chiseled abdomen. They squinted into the sun when they tried to see his face, and they each raised a hand to shield their eyes.

"I have brought you pieces for your dress," Onadesh said, dropping a small sack in front of Little Fawn.

Her eyes dropped to the sack, and she lifted the flap to reveal the small hooves of adult deer. She looked back up, blocking the sun with her hand. "Thank you." She still couldn't see his face, so she dropped her hand and pushed herself up from the ground.

His hard eyes softened when she looked into them, and they both held their breath for a moment.

"I am Little Fawn's grandmother," the old woman called from the ground, breaking the moment between Little Fawn and Onadesh. "Move away from the sun so I can see you." She waved her hand, indicating which way she wanted him to step.

Onadesh looked down at her and then obeyed, stepping to

his left.

The old woman's eyes moved up his body again, making him feel unusually uncomfortable under the scrutiny.

When she reached his face, she nodded. "You are the son of Chief Sagima."

Little Fawn looked at him in surprise, but he did not acknowledge her expression.

"Yes," he told the old woman, maintaining his rigid posture.

"Moon Wanderer is a very unusual name. Why do they call you Moon Wanderer?"

"My mother heard the name in a dream. She said The Great Creator whispered it into her ear." He hesitated. "Surely it is a part of my destiny."

She nodded and looked at him carefully. "Little Fawn says you are a warrior."

Onadesh glanced sideways at Little Fawn before looking back to the grandmother. "Yes."

"Are you a good warrior?" she asked in a worried tone. Her

quick glance to Little Fawn and then back to Onadesh told them what she feared.

He held a fist to his chest. "Yes, I am a good warrior." And then, as if to further impress the women, he said, "I am also a hunter."

The old woman nodded to the bag of hooves. "Yes, I see that." She sat silently a moment and thought before saying, "Have you yet cured the hides of these animals?"

"No, not yet," Onadesh replied.

The old woman looked to her granddaughter, who was now standing in the light, and held up a hand to shield her eyes. "Little Fawn, Onadesh was kind enough to bring you pieces for your dress. You should help him with his hides."

Little Fawn smiled at the veiled form of approval. "Yes, grandmother." Her eyes moved to Onadesh, who only nodded solemnly, looking down at her grandmother.

"I will save one for you to keep you warm this winter," he told her.

The grandmother nodded. "Thank you, Onadesh. I would appreciate that."

Onadesh looked at Little Fawn before tilting his head. "Come. My wigwam is this way."

CHAPTER 4

Little Fawn silently followed Onadesh through the Odawa camp as people bustled about doing their day's work. They wove between wigwams, fires, and racks of drying meat. Women sat weaving reed mats, and children chased each other across their path.

"This is my wigwam," Onadesh told her, pointing to a domed structure covered in large pieces of dark gray bark.

"You are very close to the chief's wigwam," she observed.

"Yes. I choose to stay close to my parents."

She nodded.

"Come." His hand brushed her lower back as he pointed to a circle of men talking.

Little Fawn felt jitters in her chest as she realized what he was doing. Obeying his command, she stepped to the circle of men.

The discussion stopped, and the chief looked up. "Yes, my son?"

"Father, this is Wa-wash-ay-wesh Koons. She has come

from Manitoulin Island with her grandmother and brother for the summer."

The chief turned to Little Fawn, his eyes studying her with interest.

"Little Fawn, this is my father, Chief Sagima."

"Welcome, Wa-wash-ay-wesh Koons," the chief greeted her as the other men watched her silently.

"Hello. Thank you." She felt unsure what else to say as she looked around the circle of older men, spotting the Midewiwin in the group.

"Wa-wash-ay-wesh Koons is a jingle dress dancer," Onadesh offered.

The chief looked at her for a long moment before nodding. "War is coming. There will be much healing for you to pray for when you next dance."

"Yes," Little Fawn agreed, her throat feeling tight.

"Little Fawn is going to help me tan the hides from my hunt."

The chief nodded solemnly. "Have you cleaned hides before?"

"I've helped my father," Little Fawn replied weakly, still feeling intimidated by the prestigious circle of eyes boring into her.

The chief nodded again. "Very well. I see you are very young. Onadesh is very accomplished. He will teach you well," he said dismissively.

Little Fawn looked to Onadesh, whose hand lightly touched her low back again, silently sending the message the discussion was over.

Turning, she quietly followed him to a large frame where the edge of the village met the forest.

"Can you sew?"

"Yes."

He scooped one of three hides up and handed it to her. "Sew this to the frame, and then we will flesh it."

She took the hide from him and spread it, fur side down, in the opening of the frame. "Are we dehairing it, too?" she asked as she punched holes through the edges with a tool fashioned from a bone that had been nearby.

"Not this one. We will save the first one for your grandmother."

Little Fawn nodded and continued to work. "The chief mentioned war."

"Yes. With the Sioux."

"They are far from us?"

"Yes, very far."

She looked around a moment, and he handed her the long leather strap. She took it from him and threaded it through one of the holes. "Must you go?"

"Yes."

"Why?" she asked with a naiveté that matched her age.

He pulled the skin taut to the edge of the frame and held it for her to sew. "If we do not go there, they will come here."

"Why?"

"Disagreement over trade routes," he said quietly.

She looped the strap through the hole and then around the edge and pulled it tight before changing her focus from the frame to the eyes of Onadesh. Their gaze held, and she felt tiny bolts of energy surge through her body. "So you must," she acknowledged in understanding.

"I must."

Her eyes drifted down to his lips briefly before returning to meet his as she blushed in embarrassment.

Breaking the silence, he cleared his throat before asking, "Have you removed the flesh before?"

Still lost in his eyes, she shook her head. "No. I have just watched my father do it."

He nodded. "I will teach you." He broke their long gaze, and Little Fawn exhaled a deep breath, realizing she had been holding it.

Onadesh looked around them, his eyes resting on a few tools laying to the side. He stood and walked over to the selection. Bending to scoop one up, he returned and held it up to Little Fawn.

"See this tool?"

She nodded.

"It is a piece of bone that has been sharpened." He took her hand and held it to the edge. "See here?"

Little Fawn carefully ran her finger along the sharp edge of white bone and nodded.

"Good. Watch me first."

He turned to the stretched hide and reached the instrument into the center. "You must first push through the flesh to the hide." He demonstrated and then looked over his shoulder to her.

Little Fawn's eyes darted from his strong back muscles that gleamed in the sunlight to the tool in his hand. "Yes, I see."

"Then you must angle the tool to cut and pull it towards you."

He demonstrated, and Little Fawn forced herself to focus on the tool as he pulled it slowly across the hide.

"If you do not angle it, you will cut the hide."

She watched him finish the strip before wiping the small

amount of flesh from the blade onto his hand.

His eyes scanned the area until he saw the dog. "Muckwa," he called.

Hearing his name, Muckwa perked his ears up from where he lay in the shade.

"Come. Food," Onadesh told him.

Muckwa trotted over and licked the warrior's hand clean before looking at him expectantly.

Onadesh turned and handed the instrument to Little Fawn.

"Try it," he told her. A flicker of humor crossed his face. "Muckwa would like some more food."

Taking the tool and leaning to reach the center of the hide, she felt his eyes burning into her, and she swallowed hard. "My arm is not long enough to reach the center."

"Then go here," he indicated to the length of her arm; and she nodded, reaching forward. She placed the instrument on the hide and timidly cut through the flesh. "Good. Now angle it, and pull it towards you," he instructed.

Little Fawn angled the instrument and timidly tried to pull it towards herself, worried she would pierce the hide.

"You must apply more pressure," he coached.

Little Fawn put a little more weight into it and pulled again. The tool cut through the flesh and then moved away from the hide.

"I do not want to pierce the hide," Little Fawn told him, frustrated.

"Here, I will guide you."

Placing an arm on each side of her to brace himself, he reached out and slid his hand over hers on the tool. Tiny surges went through her body upon his touch, and Little Fawn struggled to look at only his hand on hers.

"This is the angle," he told her as his hand tilted hers. "Now, pull it forward." His hand guided hers easily across the hide, and the bits of flesh piled against the tool. "Good, he whispered into her ear. Do not make it harder than it has to be. Do you see?"

"Yes," she croaked, unsure how to respond to his sudden closeness as his scent intoxicated her.

He lifted the tool and rubbed the side of it against his hand again, cleaning the flesh from it. Turning to Muckwa, he held out the handful of flesh; and Muckwa gently took it from Onadesh's hand. When he finished, Onadesh scratched the dog's fluffy head between the ears and turned back to Little Fawn. "You will feed him the next pull."

Little Fawn nodded, nervous she would not perform as well as she wanted to, and reached the tool over the hide again. This time she struck the correct angle with the tool and began to pull. The flesh easily separated from the hide and piled against the tool.

"I'm doing it!" she said proudly as the angle suddenly changed and the instrument pulled up, no longer doing its job.

"Yes, that is good." He took her hand again and guided it to where she had left off. "Start here and maintain your focus." He let go, and Little Fawn did as she was instructed. The flesh rose easily against the edge of the tool. When she reached the edge of the hide, she lifted the tool, glanced at him first, and rubbed the side of the blade against her hand.

Smiling proudly, she called, "Muckwa!"

Quick to learn when food was offered, Muckwa walked around Onadesh to Little Fawn and gently licked her hand clean.

Turning a gleeful smile to Onadesh, she said, "I think I can do this."

Not returning her smile, he nodded seriously. "Very good. I will work on another hide on that frame over there."

Little Fawn's smile disappeared when she realized he would no longer be working at her side. "But – but I should probably have supervision for a while longer." She looked back to the hide. "I would not want to puncture grandmother's winter wrap."

His eyes were difficult to read as he looked at her, and Little Fawn felt her cheeks warm uncomfortably.

"I will stay for one more pull, then I must work on the other hides."

Little Fawn felt a small wave of victory rush through her and tried to hide her smile as she looked back to the hide. Muckwa observed on one side and Onadesh on the other.

She cut through the flesh, turned the instrument on angle, and easily pulled it towards herself, eager to impress her audience. As her hand approached her body, his reached out and covered hers. She turned her head to look at his face so close to hers. She felt his breath on her face. Her eyes glanced down to his lips again and lingered, every cell in her body aware of the strong draw between them.

His hand tightened on hers and lifted it from the hide. For the first time, she saw a small smile cross the lips of the mighty warrior.

"You will make a good wife someday."

CHAPTER 5

Little Fawn released a loud sigh as she moved the reed basket further into the bean field and continued to pick.

"What was that about?" Dawa-Quay asked.

"I don't know," Little Fawn sighed.

"I think it is about being in love," Myinga giggled.

"You have spent a lot of time with Onadesh lately," Dawa-Quay commented.

"Yes. I'd prefer to be with him now rather than picking beans." She dropped from her squatting position onto her butt and nibbled on the end of one of the pods.

The other two girls moved their baskets closer. "Have you laid with him yet?" Myinga asked in a conspiratorial whisper.

"I would not tell others if I have."

Undeterred by her comment, Myinga plopped down next to Little Fawn, and Dawa-Quay stepped closer. "You are very young, but it will happen soon," she predicted.

"Myinga is to move to the wigwam of Running Fox when the

war party returns," Dawa-Quay told Little Fawn.

Little Fawn looked at Myinga, an impressed expression on her face. "He asked you?"

"Yes," Myinga smiled at her new friend.

"And you are excited?"

Myinga shrugged. "I think so." She looked into the blue sky above them. "Sometimes it seems so far into the future that I feel it will never happen."

"But you love him, right?" Dawa-Quay asked her friend as she joined the break in the middle of the bean field.

"Running Fox is very kind to me. Yes," she shrugged, "I guess that means I love him."

Dawa-Quay shifted her attention to Little Fawn. "And do you love Onadesh?"

Little Fawn grinned happily. "Yes, I think I do."

"How can you?" Dawa-Quay pried. "He's so serious."

"I don't think I've ever seen him smile," Myinga commented.

Little Fawn looked down at the half a bean left in her hand

and broke off a piece. "It is not often, but I have seen him smile."

"Well, you are the only one who has seen this sight," Myinga commented.

"And what have you done to make him smile?" Dawa-Quay pried again as she leaned forward with interest.

Little Fawn made an expression of surprise before tossing the piece of bean at Dawa-Quay.

"You have spent most of the summer with him, and he has not asked anything of you?" Dawa-Quay pressed.

Little Fawn whipped the rest of the bean at Dawa-Quay, who dodged the flying vegetable. "I am not telling."

Myinga watched Little Fawn with a small, knowing smile on her face. "If he has not, that means he likes her."

"It does?" Little Fawn asked naively.

"And he respects you," Myinga continued, pushing back her long, jet black hair that she held off her face with only a beaded headband around her forehead.

"If he plays his flute for you, will you say yes and move into his wigwam?" Dawa-Quay asked.

Little Fawn looked down thoughtfully and ran her fingers over the beans in her basket. Moments passed, and her friends waited patiently for an answer. Finally, Little Fawn smiled and whispered, "Yes, I would like very much to live in his wigwam."

"Of course, you are special, and maybe that is why he has not asked anything of you," Dawa-Quay pointed out.

"Who chose you to dance?" Myinga asked Little Fawn, changing the subject.

"Myself. I had a dream when I was but a small child."

"The Midewiwin did not choose you?"

Little Fawn shook her head. "My grandmother told the Mide my dream, and he told her what it meant."

"That you are chosen?" Dawa-Quay asked.

"Yes."

"And what was your dream?" Dawa-Quay inquired, crossing her legs comfortably and leaning forward with interest.

Little Fawn thought for a moment as she remembered the

dream that haunted her. "I saw myself dancing with three other women." She picked a bean from her basket and looked at it in her hands. "We wore jingle dresses and danced around a small group of sick and injured people."

"So you dreamed you were a jingle dress dancer?" Dawa-Quay repeated in summation. "That does not make you one. Why would the Mide choose you for that?"

Myinga was watching Little Fawn's face closely. "Is that all there was to your dream?"

"Yes, Wa-wash-ay-wesh Koons. We want to know, was Onadesh in it?" Dawa-Quay teased.

Little Fawn laughed dismissively and threw a piece of bean at her friend again. "No, Onadesh was not in my childhood dream."

Myinga didn't laugh as she watched her friend. "So tell us, Little Fawn, was there more to your dream?"

Little Fawn nodded and lifted the large reed basket of beans onto her lap, wishing for a distraction.

"So what was the rest of your dream?" Myinga pressed

again, still serious.

Little Fawn looked up to meet Myinga's intense stare before she whispered, "I saw myself sitting in the group of sick and injured that we danced around."

Both girls sat quietly and did not respond.

Little Fawn's sad eyes looked from one to the other before telling the final blow. "There was an arrow through my heart."

Seconds turned into minutes of silence before Dawa-Quay whispered, "Can a jingle dress dancer heal herself?"

"I do not know for certain," Little Fawn said, her eyes sad. "But, if one cannot hear the sound from the dress, I do not think they can be healed."

The other two women nodded in solemn understanding.

Myinga, watching Little Fawn carefully, asked, "And is that all that you saw in the dream?"

Little Fawn met Myinga's intense gaze with sad eyes and felt her heart beat harder in her chest. "Yes, that is all that I remember," she lied. She softly closed her eyes and dropped her head as she remembered Myinga sitting next to her in the circle of

sick and injured in her dream.

CHAPTER 6

Little Fawn rolled over and snuggled her face against the hard chest of Onadesh, searching for a tender spot to hide the tears that welled in her eyes. He wrapped an arm around her and pulled her closer to him. The cloak of trees in the ravine hung over them to hide their naked bodies.

"Was that your first time?"

"Yes," she whispered, embarrassed.

Understanding the tone of her voice, he grasped her chin between two fingers and turned it to meet his gaze. "It will get better."

Her eyes were pools of emotion as she looked at him questioningly. "Will it?"

He saw the hurt and fear in her eyes. "Yes," he replied using a gentle tone that Little Fawn had not heard from him the past month she had known him. His fingers loosened on her chin before tracing it with the tip of his index finger. "You are so delicate."

A tear escaped and ran onto her cheek. "And you are very

strong."

His eyes hardened at the realization that he had hurt her. "I will be better."

She tried to look away to hide her tear, but his hand held her face so he could watch her reactions as he spoke. "I know I can be better."

She didn't reply.

"Little Fawn, I don't want you to be with another. Give me a chance to be better."

Her mind focused on something he said. "Ever? You don't want me to be with another ever?"

"No, I do not."

"How am I to never be with another? I am only sixteen." Her voice softened before she continued. "You have seen twenty-three winters and, I'm guessing, just as many women."

Onadesh felt color rush to his face, and his jaw tightened in response.

"Am I not right?"

Not wanting her to know how close to the truth she was, he responded, "I understand your point, but I am a man. It is different for women."

She stuck out her chin defiantly. "And I am not just any woman, but I am a jingle dress dancer."

"Yes, I know."

"I do not choose to be with just one man." Her words strove to hurt him as he had hurt her. Her eyes were hard and defiant to hide her own hurt, but her voice cracked as she said it.

Muckwa let out a loud yawn from where he watched but kept his focus on the couple.

Onadesh's mind moved quickly while his eyes stayed on the prey he wanted to capture. "We are going to war soon. When I return, I would like you to move into my wigwam."

"My grandmother will never approve," she made the excuse.

"I will court you with my flute," he offered, knowing it was one of the traditions of his tribe.

She pushed away from him and sat up. "Why would I do such a thing? I am very young."

He sat up, his tall torso towering over hers. "Many women consider a great warrior to be a man who will protect and provide for them."

She crossed her arms and looked down as she spoke. "I can provide for myself, and there are other warriors I can choose to protect me." She kept her focus on the ground, hoping he wouldn't call her bluff.

Onadesh smiled a rare half smile, understanding her resistance. His voice softened. "I am a warrior and a hunter. I am strong, and my feelings for you overcame my senses. I am not accustomed to having such feelings for a woman. I will be better," he reassured her a third time.

Her face softened, but she kept her arms crossed and jutted her chin out in defiance again. "If that is so, you must prove it to me before you court me so I am able to make my decision wisely."

"Little Fawn, I would never intentionally hurt you. You know

52

how I feel about you."

She shook her head. "No, I don't. You hold your feelings inside and leave me to guess. How do I know I am not Woman Number Twenty-Four, and tomorrow you will have Woman Number Twenty-Five?"

He slipped his hand reassuringly onto her thigh. "I have not laid with another woman since I met you and Muckwa." He glanced at the vigilant dog fondly.

Little Fawn looked down at the ground between them as another thought occurred to her. The tone of her voice dropped when she asked, "What if you do not come back from war?"

A new chord of confidence rang in his voice, and he smiled a rare half smile. "I am the strongest warrior in the Odawa nation, Wa-wash-ay-wesh Koons. If you lose me, it will not be in battle."

"What if you have no choice?"

He gave his head a small shake of dismissal. "It will not happen."

"And I am to wait for you?"

"Yes."

"How long will you battle the Sioux?"

"Not many suns, but the journey across the big lake is long."

"I will not wait for you if you do not return with the war party," she lied defiantly, testing her bounds.

He smiled and leaned down to give her a kiss that lingered.

"And if I do not wait?" she continued to push.

"I will slit the throat of any man who touches you," he whispered into her ear.

Little Fawn's heart caught in her chest, realizing the serious threat; but her mind quickly forgot it when she felt an unfamiliar tingle as his hand moved slowly up her thigh.

CHAPTER 7

Kylie pulled the pan of chocolate hazelnut cupcakes from the oven and lightly tapped the top of one, watching it spring back. Satisfied, she pulled it out and sat it on the counter of her cupcake shop in downtown Harbor Springs.

"Sorry I'm late," Judy announced as she walked in the back door of the gingerbread house that served as the shop. "I don't suppose I can use traffic as an excuse in this town."

Kylie stared at the cupcakes before her and didn't respond, her hands placed expectantly on her hips.

Judy tossed her purse onto the office desk next to Cupcake and leaned to pat the puppy. "I think I'll change your name to Cake." The puppy wagged its tail happily. "You're getting much too large to be called Cupcake." She glanced at her niece, who was still staring at the pan of cooling cupcakes, and continued the conversation with Cupcake a little louder. "Well, maybe you're not a full cake yet," she leaned through the doorway, "maybe just a bowl cake." Kylie didn't respond. "Or half cake." Still no response.

"Kinda like Half Pint on *Little House on the Prairie,* only for cakes," she continued loudly as she walked up to her niece and waved a hand in front of her face.

"Anyone home?"

Kylie smiled as she broke out of her thoughts. "Yes. Sorry, Aunt Judy. Did you say something?"

"Just that I'm changing Cupcake's name to Half Cake," her aunt mumbled dismissively. She glanced down at the cupcakes that had her niece's attention. "So what's wrong with the cupcakes?"

"Huh?"

"Well, you were staring at them and ignoring me and Cupcake – I mean me and Half Cake."

Kylie smiled, finally comprehending her aunt's humor the third time around. She leaned and pushed the pan to the center of the table. "Oh, I wasn't thinking about the cupcakes." She shrugged and stepped towards the front of the store, reaching for the sandwich board to write the special on. "I was just wondering about the weird remains we found the other day."

"What about it?"

She shrugged absently. "Just who it was, how long it had been there," she ran her hands thoughtfully over the colored chalk as she spoke, "how it got there."

"I thought you said it was a dead deer."

"There was a whole pile of deer hooves, but Jason said there were also human remains."

Judy let out a grunt as she approached her niece. "First, it was probably just the dead mother of that poor baby deer that Half Cake chased down."

"And second?"

"Second," she grabbed a piece of pink chalk from the box, "it's my job to write the cupcake du jour on the board."

Kylie smiled but shook her head. "Jason said he saw hair."

"Fur."

"Long, black hair."

Judy threw her arms up. "Hallelujah, you've found the first Sasquatch remains!"

"Aunt Judy," Kylie said in a scolding tone.

"Hey, I told you there was that sighting out at Wilderness State Park."

Kylie crossed her arms and gave her aunt a look that told her she wasn't buying her story.

Judy put her hands on her hips. "So what are you thinking, a deer died on top of a person?" She held up a finger as if she had an idea. "Oh, wait, maybe the deer killed the person and dragged it to the cave to eat," her eyes wandered a moment, "or feed its family."

"It's not funny, Aunt Judy."

"No, it's not. It's ridiculous. There are no undiscovered human bodies floating around northern Michigan. This isn't New York City."

Kylie shook her head disapprovingly at her aunt. "Do you actually believe in anything?"

Judy looked into the distance thoughtfully before refocusing on her niece. "Cupcakes. I believe in cupcakes and selling enough to make my house payment every month." She lifted the piece of chalk. "So what is today's cupcake du jour?"

"It's a vanilla bean and caramel cupcake filled with bourbon-spiked apples, topped with walnut frosting and drizzled with a salted caramel sauce right before you hand it to them."

Judy blinked at her niece with a dumbfounded expression. "Good Lord, I'm going to need a bigger chalkboard," she looked at her slate thoughtfully, "maybe a billboard."

Kylie laughed. "Just write small."

"So say all that again. It was vanilla something."

Kylie opened her mouth to repeat the cupcake name when the front door opened and the handsome fire chief that also happened to have been her boyfriend for the summer stepped in.

"Hey, Sunshine," he greeted her before tipping her chin upwards with a finger and lightly kissing her.

Kylie smiled contentedly. "Mmm, good morning to you, too."

Judy cleared her throat. "Vanilla...?"

"Vanilla bean and caramel cupcake," Kylie repeated.

"Mmm, that sounds good," Jason said, "maybe I'll take some back to the station."

"Oh, there's more to it," Judy informed. "A lot more. And caramel..." she mumbled to herself as she wrote.

"So did you hear anything about the body yet?"

"Oh, did I ever hear something," he started excitedly.

"What's after 'caramel'?" Judy interrupted.

"Cupcake filled with bourbon-spiked apples." Kylie threw over her shoulder before turning back to Jason. "So what did you find out?"

"Apparently it had been there for a very long time."

"Like a year?"

"Like more than a hundred years."

"Spiked..." Judy said slowly as she wrote.

"Remains don't last that long," Kylie said dismissively.

He held up a finger. "How quickly you forget. As with the remains found in the tunnel attached to your house, a cool, damp environment is like keeping them in a refrigerator." He pretended to close a refrigerator door. "Decomposition slows down."

"Decomposition," Judy said slowly as she wrote before catching herself and erasing the word. "I mean 'apples,'" she said as she slowly wrote the word.

"Wow," Kylie whispered, remembering the ninety-year-old remains found in the mobster-built tunnel from her house that had once been Club Manitou. "So do they know who it was or how many people there were or what happened?"

"Not yet; but I would guess, from the long, black hair, it was a Native American."

"What's after 'apples'?" Judy interrupted again.

"Topped with a walnut frosting," Kylie answered without taking her eyes off of Jason. "So anything else?"

He smiled, taking joy in feeding it to her slowly and watching her reaction. "All of the deer hooves, they were left spaced on a grid, like they were laid out or something."

"Like some kind of ceremony?"

"Maybe."

"Okay, what's the last part?" Judy interrupted again. "I don't have much room left, so I might have to jot it on a Post-It note and stick it on the bottom."

Kylie glanced to her aunt as she answered, "Drizzled with a salted caramel sauce."

"Sounds messy," Judy mumbled as she wrote.

"So how do we find out?"

He flashed his long, white teeth with a small space in front, forming a dazzling grin. "We ask a Native American."

Kylie thought hard for a moment. "I don't think I know any Native Americans." Her eyes drifted up to the ceiling in thought. "Do I?" She looked back at him. "I guess I don't pay attention to that."

He stepped closer and wrapped an arm around her waist, pulling her to him. "And that's why I come in so handy."

Kylie looked delighted. "Who do you know?"

Still holding her close, he continued, "Just one of the local historians that specializes in Native American history."

"No way!"

"There's no room for the word "sauce," Judy declared. "If you really, really need it there, I'll get a Post-It, but that's the best I can do." She stepped back to look at her handiwork, and Kylie moved her eyes from Jason to her aunt for the first time since the writing started.

"Aunt Judy, no one will be able to read that without reading glasses."

"Well, maybe you should simplify things."

"Maybe you need two special boards," Jason offered.

"Maybe we need to simplify things, "Judy repeated.

"Well, I'll take a dozen back to the guys at the station later," he caught himself and looked worried, "as long as you have something unsweet for Mel."

Kylie looked down at the display case. "Hmm, why don't you take him a pear cupcake with truffle oil frosting."

Judy wrinkled her nose. "I swear, you come up with the weirdest combinations."

Kylie's smile lessened.

"Give me two of those," Jason ordered, restoring Kylie's momentary lapse of confidence.

Kylie pulled out a box and started folding the edges together. "So where do we find this historian?"

Jason glanced at his watch. "He likes to do some of his work at the coffee shop, so we might be able to catch him if you can run down the block with me."

Judy waved her arm at her niece in dismissal as she stood looking at the chalkboard disapprovingly. "You guys go, I can handle things."

"The chocolate hazelnut cupcakes still need to be frosted with the Nutella buttercream frosting." She pointed to the work table in the center of the shop. "It's all made up and ready to go."

"Yeah, yeah, I can frost," Judy replied with another wave of her hand without looking away from her handwriting on the chalkboard.

Jason held out his hand. Kylie smiled and took it as they

walked out of the shop.

"Good morning, Sam," Jason greeted Sam Shepard as he maneuvered his way up the front walk to the shop with a cane in hand.

"Morning, kids," he greeted. "Is my Buttercup in yet?"

Kylie grinned. "She is, Sam, and I'm sure she'd love to see you."

Jason gave her hand a hard squeeze, but Kylie ignored it.

"Ya don't say," he questioned with a blissful grin on his face. "Oh, seeing your Aunt Judy first thing in the morning is the best part of my day."

Jason gave her hand a hard tug, pulling her forward. "We've got to hustle."

"See you later, Sam," Kylie called over her shoulder as she took a skip and a few quick steps down the front walkway to match Jason's pace.

Kylie heard the screen door to the shop swing open followed by Sam's, "What's up, Buttercup?"

Kylie's grin widened as she heard her aunt's loud response.

"You'd better be here to buy cupcakes!"

CHAPTER 8

The canoe paddles silently hit the water and moved it behind them as the small band of warriors returned home. Onadesh sat lost deep in his thoughts as his strong, tattooed arms mindlessly moved the paddle again and again and again. In his mind, he saw the lost battle replaying over and over. He saw where their plan had failed. He saw braves he had known his entire life get their throats slit or get bludgeoned to death. He saw the moment he knew they could not win when he called out his cry of retreat.

Every time the scenes replayed in his mind, his mourning and anger grew deeper, both emotions building in him to the point he felt he would explode. When at last he spotted familiar land ahead, he threw his head back and let out a blood-curdling cry of sorrow. Seconds later, the warriors in the seven other canoes echoed his cry. "Aaaaaaaah!" came his cry of sorrow again and again, and the others continued to echo the sound.

Soon he saw curious people lining the shore, watching the

small war party return.

Lost in sorrow over the brutal deaths of a large portion of his warriors, Onadesh continued his wails, as did the other men.

Taking a deep breath and swallowing, he squinted his eyes to better see those who watched, his eyes scanning particularly for Little Fawn. "Those are not our people," he told the others as he stopped paddling to better focus on the shore.

"They are Muscodesh," Aneamishi informed his leader and friend.

"The currents have taken us too far south," Onadesh realized. "We will go closer to shore and then turn north to our village." His shaved head, except for a tuft of hair at the top, dropped back, and another wail of mourning escaped his lips. Others followed, sharing their grief with the Muscodesh.

"We will turn north now," Onadesh informed his band just before he felt something hit the side of the canoe. Before he could realize what happened, something hard and cold hit him in the arm.

"Onadesh, we are being attacked," Aneamishi informed him

from the back of the canoe.

"Why would – " he started to wonder aloud when a ball of mud, wrapped in leaves, hit his head, knocking him to the side.

A "Woot!" sounded from a canoe behind him, but this time, it wasn't a cry of sorrow, it was a cry of war.

Onadesh focused on the enemy and saw teen boys lining the shore, laughing at them and throwing rocks and mud balls. "You laugh at our mourning?" Onadesh called to them.

"You never should have gone," shouted a boy as he threw a mud ball wrapped in leaves at the mourners.

A tall, lanky boy called, "If you had stayed with your village, like we did, your warriors would not be diminished."

"Our warriors fought the Sioux while you stayed with your women," Onadesh called back. "We fought to protect our land and trade routes."

"The land we let you stay on," Aneamishi finished his friend's sentiment.

More mud balls were hurled through the air. "It is no more

your land than it is ours," called a boy.

"We know we cannot defeat the Sioux, so we are smart enough to stay here," called another Muscodesh boy.

The lanky boy threw another ball at the canoes. "And now you cry like women."

"Now you wish you had stayed with the village, like we did," taunted another boy.

"You have lost many," continued a taunt, "we are not afraid of you."

Onadesh felt the heat rise to his face as he ducked an oncoming mud ball. "We have lost many, but there are many more at the village and also on Manitoulin Island. The Odawa nation is vast and mighty."

"We are not afraid," called an especially young boy. "We will defeat you like the Sioux did, and you will cry again like women."

Aneamishi scanned the shoreline and then said, "The men and women stand behind these boys and do nothing to stop them."

Onadesh heard the anger in his friend's voice as he continued.

"They dishonor us by not respecting our mourning."

Onadesh followed his friend's gaze and saw the men standing on the shore chuckling to one another, and his face flushed with anger. Mimicking the previous canoer, he threw back his head again. This time, he did not let out a cry of mourning for his lost warriors; this time, it was a war cry.

CHAPTER 9

Little Fawn and her brown dog Muckwa stood on the edge

of the bluff and watched the canoes of men from the Odawa tribe

return to the village. Even from where she stood, she could hear

them chant. It was a chant of mourning, but there was something

else to the chant that she could not quite make out. She knew

nearly two moons ago almost twelve canoes had left. Today she

saw seven returning.

She dropped to her knees and hugged Muckwa to her.

"Please let Onadesh be with them," she prayed in a whisper.

"Please let him be with them." She buried her face in the fluffy

brown fur of the large dog. "Muckwa, pray with me. We will ask

the Great Creator to bring Onadesh back safely."

Muckwa let out a deep bark as he watched the canoes travel

along the shoreline alongside his owner.

By the time the canoes reached the shore, the entire Odawa

village stood ready to greet them. Little Fawn and Muckwa

watched from the back of the crowd.

"Welcome back, my brothers," the chief greeted solemnly as he stepped forward and placed a hand on the shoulder of his son, Onadesh, whose head hung low.

Little Fawn's heart leapt in joy and relief when she saw him.

"We have lost many," Onadesh informed him.

The chief nodded his acknowledgment as he silently counted the braves that had returned.

"They were many in number, and we were not prepared."

The chief nodded in solemn comprehension. "We will mourn the loss of our brothers tonight with a ghost dinner. Go to your families now."

Onadesh hesitated. "There is more I must tell you, Father."

The weathered chief dropped his hand from his son's shoulder. "Can it wait?"

Onadesh shook his head.

The chief solemnly nodded. "Go to your mother and Little Fawn first, and then we will speak."

The braves disbursed among the group, being greeted by

cries of joy from mothers, wives, sisters, and children.

Onadesh went first to his mother before finding Little Fawn at the back of the crowd. He did not look her in the eyes as he approached, his head hanging in shame even though his anger still burned. "We have failed."

She reached a hand to his face and lifted it so his eyes met hers. "But you have come back to me. You have come back to your one."

His eyes were empty. "But I have failed. We did not defeat the Sioux, and we have lost many." He shook his head sadly. "The Sioux fought well, and I saw so many of our warriors die." He took a slow breath and released it, pushing down his anger. "It happened so quickly, Little Fawn." He looked into her eyes. "It was terrible. I saw my childhood friends get their throats slit or receive a blow from a war club." He shook his head. "So much blood I have never seen, and so much sorrow I have never felt."

Her hand reached up to his cheek to comfort him. "It was a battle you could not have won."

"I wish I had died. I wish I did not see what I saw." His eyes looked past her. "Now, all I can think of is revenge."

"To come back to your promised is an act of bravery," she argued. She moved her body to his, wrapping her arms around his neck. "You are promised to me, not to a battle. You must keep your promise. Forget revenge."

"That is asking me to forget the blood of my brothers."

"No, it is asking you to stay with me and to have a life with me."

His arms wrapped around her waist, and his head dropped onto her shoulder for support. He inhaled the scent from her long, jet black braids and squeezed her harder.

She knew she had not convinced him. She pulled back and looked up at him. "When I dance again, I will dance for you."

His eyes clouded angrily. "You are a jingle dancer. You do not dance for me, you dance for the sick."

Her hand stroked the side of his face compassionately. "Your heart is sick."

"No." He pushed her back. "Never call my heart sick. My heart is strong." He thumped a tight fist against his chest.

She shook her head. "Your heart is weeping." She dropped a hand to his chest. "I can feel it." Her eyes widened as a new realization came over her. "Your sorrow and hatred is closing your heart."

"No, my heart is strong," he repeated defensively.

Her eyes had tears pooling in them as they looked sadly from her hand on his chest and to his eyes. "Do not close me out of your heart, Onadesh."

His hand moved up to hers and gripped it. "You were in my heart when I was born. I could not close you out even if I wanted to." She saw a hint of the old Onadesh return to his gaze as he continued. "You are a part of my heart."

She returned his grip, feeling comforted. "And you are a part of mine." She rose onto her toes to gently place a comforting kiss on the lips of her warrior. Her kiss was returned but not with the fervor she had known in the past. She stepped back. "What else is wrong?"

He was quiet for a long moment. "It is nothing."

"Tell me."

"I will speak to my father of it first."

Her eyes searched his, worried now. "Are we in danger?"

He shook his head. "Not now," he looked into the distance as he continued, "but the Muscodesh will be." He looked at her with dark eyes. "You should hide."

"What?" she felt alarmed at his sudden change in demeanor.

"If something happens, I want you to hide." His eyes wandered as his plan came together in his head before he spoke it. "Hide in our spot at the spring, and I will come for you when it is safe. Do not stay in the village."

She looked down at her feet, covered in sand. "But what will happen?"

"I am not sure, but I need to know you will be safe."

"And I will be safe there?"

He looked up as he envisioned in his mind the bluff that rose sharply on all sides of the narrow inlet, creating a spot hidden from those who did not know it was there. He nodded. "Yes, I feel you will be safe there." He bent his knees to meet her eyes. "You will be safe there, and I will find you. Yes?" He searched her eyes for her acknowledgment.

Little Fawn felt a pang of fear in her abdomen as she looked back into his eyes before nodding in silent agreement. "But what about my grandmother and brother?"

"The elderly and children will not be harmed."

"And the women?"

He looked at her, and she knew the answer before he said it. "You are different. If you are captured, you could be used as leverage against me," he hesitated, worry written all over his face now, "or worse."

"How would they know?"

"Little Fawn, we have been seen together all summer. Everyone knows how important you are to me."

Her heart warmed, and she looked up to him with adoration in her eyes. "That is good to hear."

His brows pushed together, forming two small wrinkles in the center of his forehead. "I have played my flute for you and asked you to move into my wigwam. How can you not know how I feel?"

She shrugged and smiled a small smile. "You aren't always the most expressive person. A little reassurance is always nice."

He lifted her right hand and ran his fingertips over the two white spots above her wrist that she had been born with and that had suggested her name. Focusing on the spots, he repeated with far-away eyes, "Take Muckwa with you. You will be safe there. I will find you and bring you back to my wigwam."

Her soft eyes searched his for confirmation. "Promise?"

"I will come for you." He lowered his face to hers and ran his chiseled nose along her cheek in a rare gesture of tenderness. "I promise."

CHAPTER 10

Little Fawn spun around excitedly in her dress as her grandmother looked on.

"Shh," she quieted the twirling young woman. "You must not make the sound until you dance in the dress."

Little Fawn nodded soberly, realizing her error. She ran her hands lightly over the hooves and bits of antlers attached to the dress and remembered the prayers she had prayed each day for the last year over each piece before attaching it to the dress.

"You are lucky Onadesh is such a mighty hunter. You would not have so many pieces to your dress were he not," her grandmother acknowledged.

Little Fawn nodded again, her fingertips lightly gliding over the pieces as she remembered Onadesh and his advice. "I should have danced last night," she told the older woman.

"Last night was the ghost supper," her grandmother commented. "You will dance tonight."

"Will I? Or will some other reason arise that I cannot?"

The older woman's eyes clouded over. "Have you seen something, my child?"

Little Fawn's fingertips continued to move lightly over the pieces on the dress as her mind wandered before looking at the other woman. "I just have a feeling that I will never dance in my dress, grandmother."

If the older woman felt panic, she did not show it but only nodded.

The somber conversation was interrupted by a little boy who poked his head into the wigwam. "There is a war council!"

Little Fawn drew in her breath sharply. "Now?"

"Yes." Her little brother held out his hand to her. "Come watch with me from the tree, Little Fawn."

Little Fawn looked at her grandmother with large eyes, and her grandmother looked back with eyes that told her granddaughter she understood her prediction.

"Come," said her brother, still holding out his hand to her, "it's already started."

Little Fawn bowed her head in respect to her grandmother before stepping from the wigwam and letting the little boy lead her towards the sound of drums that now played.

The crowd of tribal members was large, and Little Fawn could not see.

She felt an insistent tug on her hand. "From our tree, Little Fawn."

"I'm too old to climb trees now, Ojig," she bent and whispered back to the boy named for an otter. Her eyes caught the pieces on her dress out of the corner of her eye. "Besides, I cannot ruin my dress."

He paused his tug and gestured to the crowds. "But we will never be able to see anything here, and the war council will not have you dance tonight."

Little Fawn knew he was right as her eyes scanned the crowd for an opening that didn't exist.

"Come," Ojig urged again. "We will miss it if you don't."

Giving in to his insistence, she let him lead her around the crowd and to a large pine tree at the edge. She watched as her brother scampered up the tree before looking back at her.

"Hurry, Little Fawn," he whispered.

Taking great care not to damage her dress, Little Fawn climbed the tree with the same ease she always had, not stopping until she was high above the crowd. Below her was a fire surrounded by the chief, Midewiwin, and braves. Women, children, and the elderly stood on the outside of the circle. Drums played hypnotically as she heard the chief speak.

"There was a time when the Odawa lived here without the Muscodesh. When they came here, homeless, we took pity on them. We said, 'We have plenty. There are many fish in the lakes, many fish in the rivers. There are many animals for food, and the crops grow plentifully.' We let them live here, and we have all lived together peacefully until now."

Little Fawn felt a shiver run up her spine.

"Earlier this summer, two Muscodesh killed one of our women as she tended to crops in a field." Murmurs floated up from the crowd before the chief continued. "Yesterday, as our warriors returned in mourning, the Muscodesh youth mocked our warriors and threw stones and balls of mud at their canoes."

More murmurs floated up from the crowd. Little Fawn looked at the boy next to her in the tree with wide eyes. "I do not like where this is going," she whispered to Ojig, who shook his head in agreement.

The drums pounded into the night as the chief continued solemnly. "The Muscodesh do not respect the Odawa and are no longer welcome here." Murmurs of agreement came from the crowd. "The Odawa leaders have met in council and made a decision." He paused for emphasis. "Tonight the Muscodesh will cease to exist."

Little Fawn drew in her breath sharply as whoops erupted from the warriors and the surrounding crowds.

"Tonight we leave, and we attack at daybreak while the Muscodesh are still asleep." The chief's words seemed to linger heavily in the air and left a feeling of dread. He lifted an arm and

pointed it to half of the warriors. "You will attack from the south."
He turned to the other half of the warriors. "As the Muscodesh are driven north, you will be waiting there for them."

More whoops erupted from the painted warriors as the chief dropped his head and began to chant.

"I must stop Onadesh," Little Fawn whispered to her brother as she started to climb down the tree.

"He is a warrior. He will not listen to you," the boy reminded her.

Little Fawn thought back to Onadesh's last words to her, and she felt a wave of relief sweep over her. "Yes, he will. I will go to our spot, and he will find me."

"He is going to war now."

"And I am leaving now."

CHAPTER 11

Onadesh stands for Moon Wanderer and, true to his name,
Onadesh led his warriors through the dark night to the Muscodesh
village. Their tattooed bodies were painted with war paint. The
short tufts of hair left at the top of their shaved heads kept their
vision clear and gave their enemies little to grab on to. Their loin
cloths had knives and tomahawks strapped at their hips, and their
hands held war clubs.

"This battle is not right," Aneamishi whispered into his
friend's ear as they began the walk that would take the entire night.

"Yes, it is," Onadesh insisted. "You were there. You saw
them mock us. You know how they killed poor Myinga for no
reason as she worked in a field of crops. They have lost their
respect for us. They have forgotten how we gave them a home
when they had none."

"But it was the young boys, not the entire tribe," Aneamishi
said.

"But the entire tribe stood by and watched them mock our

mourning," Onadesh said, stopping to look at his friend. "There was no trial held for the men who murdered Myinga. They have no justice system, so we must give them justice."

"But the women and children? We have never killed women and children before. We usually bring them back to the village to be absorbed into the tribe."

"We have enough mouths to feed, and their tribe has grown very large. We cannot take in thousands."

Aneamishi looked taken aback. "Have they grown to that many?"

"Very possibly. Maybe more."

"I cannot kill women and children."

Onadesh set his jaw. "Do it with compassion."

Aneamishi swallowed hard.

"The young men who mocked us will not be so lucky," Onadesh muttered before again starting the trek towards the Muscodesh village.

"What if we do not fare well?"

Onadesh let out a grunt. "We are many more in number, and we will catch them while they sleep. We will fare well."

"Attacking as they sleep is cowardly. It is not fair."

Onadesh continued to look straight ahead as he spoke. "This battle was started by cowards."

Many minutes ticked by in silence as the two warriors led the band behind them through the dark forest before Aneamishi spoke again. "When this is finished, will you finally fulfill your promise to Little Fawn?"

Onadesh didn't look at his friend as he replied. "Yes. After our battle, there will be a victory feast. The following night will be our wedding feast, and I will move her into my wigwam."

Aneamishi nodded. "And have you thought of what will happen to her if you do not return from this battle?"

Onadesh snapped his head to look at his friend. "There is no doubt in my mind that I will return to her. I have made her a promise, and I intend to keep it."

"But suppose you do not. Nodan offered her grandmother

semmar to smoke while you were fighting the Sioux. Maybe he will step to your place if you are not back."

"Enough!" Onadesh grabbed his friend loosely by the throat to send his message home. "It will take more than tobacco to turn Little Fawn or her grandmother's head." He pushed his friend back hard. "I told you that I know I will survive this battle and get back to her. Little Fawn and I have a plan, and we will safely meet." He turned to start his march through the darkness again, his war club clutched tightly in one hand. "Keep your mind on the task at hand, and do not anger me again."

Aneamishi rubbed his neck with his free hand before he fell silently into step behind his friend.

Minutes before sunrise, Onadesh, Aneamishi, and half of the Odawa nation stood on the north side of the Muscodesh village beside the doors of the wigwams. Seconds of silence ticked by before Onadesh issued a blood-curdling war cry that was quickly echoed by a similar cry from the south side.

The Muscodesh men rushed out of wigwams first and met a

quick demise. If the women and children did not follow to meet a similar fate, fire was set to the wigwams. Mass chaos erupted, and Onadesh saw people covered in blood and running hysterically around him. Some of them began to make it to the forest and disappear into the morning dusk.

"Aneamishi, many are escaping to the forest!" Onadesh called to his friend.

Aneamishi swung his war club at a head and watched a man fall to the ground who had been shielding his wife and children. "Aaaaah!" Aneamishi screamed as he delivered similar fates to the woman and children.

"Aneamishi, come!" Onadesh called his friend.

Aneamishi turned to respond to his friend and felt a knife tear through his upper back. "Aaaaah!" he cried in shock as he turned to see a young woman looking at him with more hate in her eyes than he had ever seen. "Aaaaah!" he screamed again as he swung his war club at her, knocking her to the ground.

"Aaaaah!" he screamed in both pain and frustration with his

task.

"Come!" Onadesh called again.

"Aaaaah!" Aneamishi screamed again as he felt vast amounts of blood running down his back.

Onadesh ran to his friend and pulled the knife from his back before turning to plunge it into a warrior coming at him. "I will get the otter skin bag of medicine from the Midewiwin," he informed his friend. "He will heal you."

Aneamishi nodded in pain.

"Come, many are getting away," Onadesh gestured towards the forest.

"We must finish alongside our brothers here before we chase the few, Onadesh."

Onadesh looked at the groups flocking into the forest and then at the carnage all around him. He nodded and let out another war cry as he attacked another wigwam.

CHAPTER 12

Jason led Kylie by the hand through the front door of the bustling coffee shop at the base of the State Street hill. He paused his step to search the crowds, and Kylie scanned the tables of tourists, wondering which looked the most like a historian.

"This way," he said as he gave her hand a tug that urged her to follow him.

They wove through the crowds until she heard her boyfriend call, "Aaron, how ya doing?"

A muscular Native American man sitting next to a back window in a quiet corner looked up and smiled with recognition. Standing to extend his hand, he said, "Jason, hello. It's been a while, my friend. How are you?"

Jason gave the man's hand a solid shake. "Good, I'm good." He pulled Kylie forward with his hand that still held hers. "Kylie, this is Aaron Redfeather. He happens to be our local historian on Native American history."

Kylie pushed one of her short, blonde strands of hair behind her ear, grinned a dimpled grin, and shook Aaron's hand. "Nice to meet you."

"Have a seat," Aaron offered, gesturing to the other side of the table he sat at with his laptop.

Jason waved at the barista, holding up two fingers and pointing to their table before sitting down.

"So what brings you two in? I've never seen you here."

Kylie leaned forward excitedly. "Jason thinks he found a body, and it was really weird because – "

Jason held up a hand to silence her and cleared his throat. "This is official business. Let me explain." Kylie leaned back as he thought a moment and then began, "We were out on Lower Shore Drive, and her dog came upon what was left of a body."

"That's what I said," Kylie whispered to herself.

Aaron looked relaxed. "Wow, that's really interesting; but why are you telling me this?"

Kylie bit her lip as Jason continued.

"The only thing that looked like human remains was some

long, black hair."

Aaron's face clouded over. "So you think it may be remains of a Native American?"

"Exactly," Kylie jumped in, unable to contain herself.

Jason held up a hand to silence her again, and she crossed her arms and let out an exasperated sigh, jutting out her lower lip to blow a short strand of blonde hair off of her forehead.

Jason leaned in to keep others from hearing before continuing in a hushed tone. "The other thing that we found with the body were a bunch of deer hooves."

"Deer hooves?" Aaron echoed thoughtfully.

Jason nodded. "They weren't piled up or anything, but they were kind of laid out in a grid, almost as if they had at one time been attached to one another."

"Or maybe they were a part of some sort of ceremony," Kylie interrupted, unable to help herself.

Aaron nodded solemnly. "How old do they think the body is?"

"They're running DNA tests, but well over a hundred years old."

Aaron nodded again in comprehension. "Was this near the church on Lower Shore Drive?"

Kylie pinched her lips tightly together in an effort to keep from contributing to the story.

"Not far from it. It was in a tiny cave at the base of Devil's Elbow." When Aaron didn't offer any insight, he asked, "Is there a burial ground there or something?"

Aaron crossed his arms. "There have been no archeological findings there."

Kylie felt her heart sink. "Could the little cave be a burial spot?"

Aaron shrugged. "Anything is possible."

"What do you think about the deer hooves?" Jason asked as the barista slipped two lattes in front of the couple.

Aaron leaned back against the cushion of the booth, his arms still crossed. "The part of your story that interests me is that you say the hooves seemed to be laid out in a grid."

"Yes," Jason commented. "They weren't piled randomly but were perfectly spaced on the ground."

Aaron nodded thoughtfully. "What I believe you have found is something holy among the Odawa people."

"Holy?" Kylie echoed. "Like a burial ground?"

Aaron shook his head. "Like the remains of a jingle dress dancer."

Kylie's eyes widened with interest, and she glanced at Jason before leaning forward and whispering, "What's a jingle dress dancer?"

Aaron's expression was solemn as he looked at the couple across from him. "To explain that to you, I must tell you the story of the first jingle dress dancer."

"I have time," Kylie told him, forgetting her shop for the moment and wrapping her hands around the warm cup in front of her.

Jason's right arm slipped comfortably over the back of

Kylie's chair as Aaron nodded.

"So you want to hear about the legend of the jingle dress."

Kylie nodded, and Jason smiled, humored by her intense interest.

Aaron took a deep breath and let it out slowly. "A very long time ago, there was a great sickness that washed over the land of the Odawa. The entirety of the people were sick, the land was sick, and even the animals were sick."

"There was a young girl in an Odawa village, and she and her family prayed to The Creator for a solution to heal her people." He reached for his cup of coffee and took a sip before continuing. "One night, The Creator sent her a vision in a dream. What the girl saw was this kind of dress that no one had ever seen before."

"That's the jingle dress?" Kylie interrupted.

Aaron nodded. "When the girl woke up the next day, she told her grandmother about her dream. The girl and her grandmother worked together to create the dress."

"By collecting deer hooves?" Kylie interrupted again.

"Not at once," Aaron replied. "Over the next year, she would use one hoof every day. They would pray over this hoof, putting the prayer into it, and then attach it to the dress."

"So there were three hundred sixty-five hooves attached to this dress?" she asked, looking to Jason for confirmation of what he'd seen.

"Sounds about right," Jason commented, remembering the scene inside the cave.

"Sounds like a heavy dress," Kylie muttered.

"Yes, it was," Aaron agreed. "The children that were jingle dress dancers had lighter dresses with less pieces on them. Receiving a dress with the full three hundred sixty-five pieces was a sign of becoming an adult."

"So were all women jingle dancers?" Kylie asked.

Aaron shook his head. "No."

"So how did they decide to become one?"

Aaron sipped his coffee thoughtfully before looking directly at Kylie. "Being a jingle dancer is not something you choose; it chooses you."

Kylie nodded, infatuated with the story. "So how did the dress work?"

Aaron set his cup down. "At the powwow the next year, the girl wore the dress. When she danced, the dress made a 'shook, shook, shook' noise." He made the sound pushing air through his teeth. "It was a sound no one had ever heard before. When one heard the noise from the dress, they were healed of their illness."

"Wow," Kylie commented.

"To this day, it is a very holy dress. It is a sacred thing."

"People still wear them?" Jason asked.

Aaron nodded. "But, once there was contact with Europeans, they no longer used hooves. Instead, they used the peeled lids from tobacco tins. You can actually go to a powwow today and find people giving tobacco to jingle dress dancers. They ask them, while they dance, to pray for loved ones with illnesses or for their own illnesses, addiction, things like that."

"Wait," Kylie interrupted his story. "So you're saying what

we found are the remains of a jingle dress dancer pre European contact?"

Aaron just looked at her with a blank expression.

"That's not possible. Nothing could exist that long."

"Refrigerator," Jason reminded her.

"Even that wouldn't keep something that long," Kylie commented.

"What you found is holy and sacred to my people," Aaron told her. "Perhaps it is there for a reason, and perhaps you were meant to find it."

Kylie felt a shiver ripple up her spine. "So what would be the reason a jingle dress dancer would want us to find her?"

Aaron shrugged. "Isn't the reason any spirit lingers completion of unfinished business?"

CHAPTER 13

Little Fawn's moccasins padded softly on the dirt foot path as she followed Muckwa at a slow jog. She had not had time to change, and her jingle dress now jingled eerily and inappropriately in the night. After the warriors had left, she and Ojig had waited in the tree for the crowd to clear before coming down. Women were bustling about, and the voices of many kept the sounds of the night at bay.

"Grandmother will be angry if you leave while the men are at battle," Ojig had warned her when they finally climbed down undetected and stood at the edge of the village.

Little Fawn gave him a tight hug. "I know. That is why I must leave now, instead of from the wigwam."

"Can't you wait until morning?" her little brother asked.

Little Fawn shook her head. "Onadesh wants me to wait for him at our secret spot. He will find me on the way back from the Muscodesh village."

Ojig looked worried.

She knelt down, her hands on his arms. "Would you like to come with me?"

His eyes looked into the dark forest surrounding the village and listened to the sounds of the night. "No," he shook his head, "and I don't want you to go either."

Little Fawn tried to think of something to cheer him. "In a few nights, we will have my wedding feast, and I will join Onadesh in his wigwam."

"Then I will be the oldest in our wigwam," he said, pointing a proud thumb at his chest as he puffed it out. His happiness paused for a moment. "I mean after grandmother," he corrected himself.

"Yes, you will. It will be your job to take care of grandmother. Is that something you think you can do?"

"Yes," he replied. "I have been hunting with Onadesh, and he has taught me well. I will be the provider and the man of our wigwam."

His doting sister smiled as she pushed some hair off of his cheek. "Yes, you will, and I know you will provide well. So now you must begin by providing for me. Run and fetch me some dried meat and berries to take with me."

As she ran, the muted thuds of her moccasins and the gentle jingles of her dress were the only sounds as she moved quickly through the moonlit forest.

"I'm glad you're here, Muckwa," she told the large dog as she heard a bird screech and a shiver ran up her spine. She slowed her pace and strained her eyes to see into the darkness. "I did not realize how many bends in this path there are," she told Muckwa as she walked along the edge of the steep bluff, looking for the inlet where she and Onadesh often met when they wanted to have some privacy.

"I think it's this one," she told Muckwa as she took a left off of the foot path and headed into the tight ravine and away from the waters of the big lake.

Working her way through the underbrush, she finally located the small pool at the back of the ravine. Pulling a blanket from her bag, she spread it in a clearing between the pool of water and the back of the bluff.

Muckwa crawled onto the edge of the blanket and laid down as Little Fawn plopped down next to him, tired from the excitement. She pulled a piece of dried meat out of the bag and gave it to the dog as she ran her hands through his thick, brown fur and let out a sigh. "I have lain here many times with Onadesh, but tonight I lay here with you," she told the dog.

Muckwa let out a whimper and dropped his head onto his large paws.

"I know, I'm tired, too," she told the dog as she curled up next to him and put her head next to his. "Onadesh will be here by morning, and he will take us home." She continued to stroke his thick fur. "Do not worry, Muckwa, I will bring you with me when I move into his wigwam. It will be a new home for both of us, and we will always be together."

Muckwa's eyes scanned the forest for danger as his owner snuggled closer to him and drifted off to sleep.

CHAPTER 14

Onadesh and Aneameshi ran at the back of the war party as they herded the terrified Muscodesh through the forests, leaving a trail of bodies behind. As they ran north, Onadesh realized that the Muscodesh were heading back towards their village, and he felt a wave of relief surge through his body. Little Fawn was hidden away safely. No Muscodesh would harm her or hold her hostage. He had safely hidden the thing most important to him.

"The sun is setting. We must stop for food and rest," Aneamishi told Onadesh.

"We cannot stop. If we do, they will escape us."

"We cannot completely wipe out the tribe," Aneamishi argued. "There are only a few hundred left. We can absorb them into the village"

Onadesh looked at his friend as they walked through the forest, Aneamishi's wound slowing him considerably from the rest of the war party. "You want a wife?"

Aneamishi shrugged and touched his hand to the aching

gash in his back. "A wife and a family," he winced in pain, "if I make it back."

Onadesh slapped his hand gently on his friend's shoulder. "You will, my friend."

Aneamishi took in his surroundings. "We are already very close to our village."

Onadesh nodded. "Yes, and the Muscodesh journey will end there." Onadesh's focus turned to the left as he heard a stick snap loudly, and he relaxed when he saw the runner wave an arm at them.

"We are herding the last of the Muscodesh into one of the ravines in the cliff," the runner informed the two. "Their demise will be quick."

Onadesh pushed his friend forward, his arm still on his. "Get the medicine man. Have him come meet us. Tell him Aneamishi needs his help."

The runner took in the grim appearance of Aneamishi, who was moving at a slow pace and hunched over. His eyes grew dark as he nodded in understanding before disappearing into the forest.

"Go ahead, my friend," Aneamishi told Onadesh. "Go finish this war so we may resume our life we were meant to have."

"I cannot leave you," Onadesh told him.

Aneamishi indicated to the forest around him. "We are very close to our land. The Midewiwin will find me," he told him, referring to one of the medicine men.

Onadesh looked around. "It is getting dark, I cannot leave you."

Aneamishi's posture drooped further. "I must rest. The Midewiwin will find me," he repeated. He gestured a dismissal with his hand. "Go, go. Do not leave our brothers to fight alone."

Onadesh hesitated only a moment as his eyes scanned the dusky forest. "Very well. You rest, and I will see you back at the village."

Aneamishi nodded as he dropped to sit on a large log.

Onadesh's eyes took in the blood that covered the tattoos on the entire back side of his friend from the wound. He felt concern for his childhood friend yet didn't want to desert his fellow warriors in their battle. He dropped a hand to Aneamishi's shoulder. "I will see you soon, my brother."

Aneamishi nodded weakly.

Onadesh took a long look at his friend before disappearing into the dusk-covered forest, his moccasins treading silently over the leaves as his paint-covered body disappeared from Aneamishi's view.

Onadesh knew he was nearing the ravine when he heard the terrified screams intermixed with the whoops of warriors as they conquered the unsuspecting tribe that had mocked the Odawas in mourning.

Onadesh felt a wave of relief as he counted the ravines in the near darkness and knew that Little Fawn was safe in their spot. Before him he saw a thousand Odawa warriors covering the mouth of one of the ravines. The screams from victims inside reached his ears, and he knew they were defenseless against their massacre.

"Here, use this quiver of arrows and this bow," Nakoma told

him as he approached. "The opening is too narrow, and there are too many Odawa between us and the Muscodesh. We will never get to the front to use our war clubs."

Onadesh pulled an arrow from the quiver, aimed it at one of the terrified faces in the ravine on the other side of the Odawa warriors, and released it. To his satisfaction, the person was struck and fell to the ground. Encouraged, he reached into Nakoma's quiver again, drew another arrow, and aimed at another face in the dusk. As he released the arrow, he saw the face turn towards him, and recognition swept over him as the arrow soared through the masses of people and reached its target. Onadesh drew in a sharp gasp as he felt his heart stop.

CHAPTER 15

"So," Kylie concluded as she took another sip of her latte, "there is nothing else you know about Devil's Elbow?"

Aaron shook his head, his strong arms still crossed over his chest comfortably. "Just rumors. Nothing that is substantiated." He shrugged, "And then, of course, what people tell me at the lectures I give."

Kylie leaned forward, interested again. "What do people tell you at lectures?"

He shrugged again, this time dismissively. "Just that they think Devil's Elbow is haunted."

Her eyes widened. "By the jingle dancer?"

He reached for his cup of coffee. "Who knows," he responded, lifting the cup to his lips.

"Well, why do they think it's haunted?"

He took a slow sip and set the cup down. "Many say they hear voices at night."

"Voices?"

"And a drum," he continued.

"An Indian drum?"

He nodded. "And many people have seen things."

"Like ghosts?"

He shrugged again, obviously not giving this information much weight. "Apparitions, or sometimes they just catch something out of the corner of their eye."

Kylie was quiet for a moment as she thought and remembered a childhood ghost story she had heard. "Anything about a man with a satchel looking for a ride?"

Aaron chuckled and wrapped his hands around the warm cup. "Nothing that specific."

"So, if they hear voices," Kylie's mind was processing the new information, "that's plural." Aaron just stared at her. "More than one."

"Yes."

Kylie looked at Jason, whose arm still rested comfortably across the back of her chair. He scrunched his eyebrows together and gave his head a tiny shake, so she continued.

"Well, the jingle dress dancer we found is only one. 'Voices' is plural. Who would she be speaking to, or who else would be there?"

For the first time, Aaron looked uncomfortable and turned his focus to his cup. "There is another story about Devil's Elbow," he told the couple.

"Besides the strange sightings?" Kylie asked.

Aaron nodded his head. "There is a theory that it was the sight of a massacre."

"Massacre?" Kylie had an appalled look on her face.

Aaron nodded again.

"We would have heard about that, or artifacts would have been found at the location," Jason told the historian.

"You would think," Aaron agreed. "Do you want to hear the story?"

"Do all good cupcakes have frosting?" Kylie asked.

Both men looked at her with blank expressions.

She blushed. "Yes. That means yes."

"To fully understand the story, I must start from the very beginning."

Jason raised three fingers to the barista and then made a circular motion towards their table. She nodded back to him in understanding.

Aaron swallowed and looked into the eyes of his audience. "At one time, all of this land belonged to my people."

"Before Europeans," Kylie filled in.

"Yes." He closed his laptop to focus on his story. "One day, another tribe, who had traveled very far, came to the Odawa. They were the Muscodesh. They were cave dwellers from the Great Plains, and they had lost their home. My people told them, 'We have plenty of land. The rivers have many fish, and the lakes are plentiful. We will share our land with you and welcome you.' And so the Muscodesh made a life here and stayed."

"Then they got cocky and killed the nice Odawas who let them stay here?" Kylie interrupted. She felt Jason's hand nudge her shoulder.

Aaron shook his head. "No, not at all. They lived together peacefully for many years."

"So what changed?" Kylie asked.

"The Odawa were mighty warriors. One day they were returning home from war, probably in Wisconsin."

The barista set three fresh drinks in front of the group. Aaron took a cup and another sip before continuing. "The warriors had lost many in battle and were letting out loud cries and wails of mourning from their canoes. Some of the Muscodesh saw the mourners and began to mock them. Soon, they threw rocks at them and jeered."

"How rude," Kylie commented as she held her cup near her lips to smell the sweet scent of the latte.

Jason gave her another nudge to be quiet, and she threw him a rebellious look.

"This did not set well with the Odawa. They returned to their village both angered and humiliated."

"So then they went to war over a little name calling?" she interrupted again.

Aaron shook his head. "It was more than that. Earlier in the spring, one of the Odawa women had been working in the fields."

"Because the women were the farmers, right?" Jason interrupted.

"Yes," Aaron confirmed. "This Odawa woman was very beautiful. Two Muscodesh braves were passing by and noticed her. They hid in the bushes and watched her until the other women returned to the village."

"I have a bad feeling about this," Kylie commented.

"When the woman was alone in the field, the two braves approached her."

"This wasn't our jingle dancer, was it?" she asked in a worried tone.

"No," Aaron confirmed. "When the woman would not yield to the requests of the young braves, a fight ensued, and it was not long before the two men strangled her."

"Yikes," Kylie shivered.

"The Muscodesh braves were not held accountable for the death of the woman, and tension began to rise between the tribes."

"So the jeering was kind of the straw that broke the camel's back?" Kylie said.

"Yes. The Odawa returned to their village and held a war council. That night, they traveled to the Muscodesh village and attacked while they slept."

"Ugh, that's harsh," Kylie commented, and Jason chuckled softly at her involvement in the story. "So how does that get us to Devil's Elbow?"

Aaron took another sip from his cup before setting it on the table in front of him and pushing up his thin glasses. "Legend has it that the Muscodesh that were not killed in the village were herded into the ravine of Devil's Elbow. Here, they were trapped and massacred."

Kylie shuddered. "What did they do with the children when all of the parents were killed?"

A shadow swept over Aaron's face before he continued. "The children were killed, too."

No one had a comment as the group sat in silence and absorbed this news.

"They killed children?" Kylie finally whispered.

Aaron nodded, not appearing proud of the story.

"So why isn't Devil's Elbow some kind of sacred memorial area?" she asked.

"Because that's just a legend."

"Sounds pretty real to me," she commented, taking a sip from her cup.

"There have been no artifacts found there to prove anything ever happened there at all."

"Until now," Kylie added to the story.

"One dead jingle dress dancer does not account for the massacre of an entire tribe," Aaron said solemnly.

"They killed the whole tribe?" she asked.

He nodded.

"How is that possible? Not one single person got away?"

Aaron's eyes dropped to his cup with his hands wrapped around it, absorbing its warmth and comfort. He didn't look up from the cup as he said, "This legend is special because it is the only time in the annals of Native American History where an entire tribe of people has been completely wiped from existence."

CHAPTER 16

Myinga stood from her work in the rice marshes and threw her long, dark hair off of her face.

"No breaks, Myinga," Dawa-Quay told her friend as she took the vessel of water off of her shoulder and poured it over the wild rice. "Tomorrow is your marriage ceremony to Running Fox, and you will not have time for work in the morning."

Myinga sat in a dry spot in the rice and dropped her head against her hand. "The Midewiwin said he had a dream about me, and marrying Running Fox is not my destiny."

"Well, something had better change pretty quickly," Little Fawn interrupted the two. "Your destiny happens tomorrow."

"Maybe dreams and visions aren't real," Myinga said with a sigh as she scanned the forest surrounding them. "Maybe our destiny is whatever and whoever we choose."

"Well, I shall marry Onadesh shortly after you marry Running Fox," Little Fawn informed. "Then we shall each have a similar destiny."

"And children that will play together," Dawa-Quay followed up as her hands continued to work.

Little Fawn stared at her friend who gazed dreamily into space. "Do you not love Running Fox?" she asked.

Myinga shrugged. "Of course I do, Wa-wash-ay-wesh Koons," she called Little Fawn in their native tongue. "I just have a feeling that something is going to happen."

Dawa-Quay threw a handful of wild rice at her friend. "Of course you do. Tomorrow you will be sharing a blanket and a wigwam with Running Fox."

The girls giggled. "I suppose that might be what I have this odd feeling about," Myinga laughed as she returned to her work. I just feel – "

A branch snapped loudly behind the young women, and they all turned towards the sound and froze. Seconds turned into minutes as no one moved.

"There are no bird sounds," Myinga whispered to her friends as they stood frozen.

"Maybe it was a mika," Little Fawn offered.

Myinga shook her head solemnly. "A raccoon would not make such a large sound, and they are nocturnal."

"A deer?" Dawa-Quay offered.

"Maybe," Myinga whispered to her friends.

The young women stood frozen, listening and watching for a long time.

"I think it has gone," Myinga told them, her eyes still watchful.

No one moved.

Finally, Little Fawn exhaled loudly. "It is getting late. We should get back to the village."

Myinga stood staring into the forest. "You two go back. I will finish up here and follow you."

"We will all finish," Dawa-Quay told her.

Myinga broke her gaze with the forest to turn to the younger girls. "I would like some time alone before I marry Running Fox," she told them. "I will finish up in a few moments and be right behind you."

"There is only one section left," Little Fawn told her. "We can finish it quickly."

"It is nothing," Myinga dismissed. "My thoughts and I would like to finish it alone."

Dawa-Quay grinned at her friend. "Just make sure you follow us, Myinga. Do not run away with your destiny the Mide told you about."

Myinga's eyes darkened. "Growing old with Running Fox and my friends is my destiny. You will not lose me."

Now Little Fawn smiled at her friend. "You're not afraid of going to Running Fox's wigwam, are you?"

Myinga smiled at the jab meant to elicit more information. "I have known Running Fox long enough to have a fairly good idea what to expect in that department."

Little Fawn leaned closer to her friend. "But you will tell us what happens, right? Onadesh wants me to move into his wigwam, and I would appreciate your information."

Myinga smiled mysteriously at her friends. "What happens between a man and woman in their wigwam is sacred. It is not to be shared."

Little Fawn narrowed her eyes. "Sacred or fun?"

"Fun? It's fun?" Dawa-Quay asked with large, virginal eyes.

Myinga smiled quietly. "You will find out when your time comes, Dawa-Quay. Now go back with Wa-wash-ay-wesh Koons. I will follow shortly."

Myinga heard a rustle from the forest beyond and coughed loudly to hide the noise from the other girls. "You must go now. Give me my time to think before I move into a new wigwam."

"Very well." Little Fawn bent and scooped up the large, empty water vessel and placed it onto her shoulder.

Dawa-Quay hesitated, her eyes scanning the forest. "Do not be long, or we will send Running Fox for you."

Myinga smiled at her friends. "I promise, I will not be long."

As the other women disappeared into the forest on the opposite side of the field, Myinga began her work on the final section of wild rice, the wet ground under her chilling her feet. Humming to herself, she worked down one side of the remaining area and turned to finish the other side when her eyes caught a glimpse of two figures standing at the edge of the marsh.

Standing to her full height, she held her chin up proudly as they walked towards her without speaking.

"Who are you?" one of the men asked.

Still holding her chin high, she answered, "I am Myinga of the Odawa and am promised to the mighty hunter Running Fox."

The men nodded, taking in the information as their eyes watched her carefully.

"Who are you?" Myinga asked in return.

"It does not matter who we are," one of the men told her.

Myinga squinted her eyes to look at them more carefully. "Maybe you are my destiny," she whispered to herself.

"You speak to me?" one asked, stepping forward and running the back of his hand over her cheek.

Myinga stood her ground. "I was speaking to myself."

He nodded, and his eyes moved over her body before returning to her face. "You are very beautiful."

Myinga did not respond to his inappropriate comment and touch.

The second man craned his neck to scan the horizon. "Where have your friends gone?"

Myinga thought quickly before speaking. "They went to get Running Fox to carry the water vessels for me. He will be here any minute."

The first man smiled a knowing smile. "It is getting dark. I do not believe you." He reached his hand to touch her face again, and Myinga ducked away from him as the second man moved in behind her.

"I think you might like to visit my wigwam tonight," the first man commented, moving in closer as his partner held Myinga in place by the shoulders."

"I am already promised to another," Myinga told him.

"And what a foolish man that is to leave such a beautiful

woman in the fields alone," the aggressor commented as he moved closer, grabbed her arm, and ran his tongue up her cheek.

"Running Fox will kill you for that," Myinga told him as she struggled to free herself from the other.

The man let out a deep chuckle. "He will have to find you first." He touched his tongue to her lips this time. "If you're good, I may keep you in my wigwam."

"And if I'm not?" Myinga spat at him as panic coursed underneath her tough exterior.

His hands wrapped around her waist, and she felt him press against her. "Then you may have to stay in the wigwam of Singing Bird," he said, gesturing to the man that held her.

Disgusted by their behavior and feeling panic turn to terror, Myinga spat in the first man's face before bending her knee up to his groin to deliver a driving blow.

The first man went down in pain as Singing Bird grabbed at her throat as he stood behind her. "I like a woman with a battle in her," he whispered into her ear.

Myinga swung her right elbow around hard, knocking it into Singing Bird as she let out a scream for help.

Singing Bird's grip on her throat tightened until her air flow became restricted and panic, fear, and realization all filled Myinga's eyes.

The first man, recovering from his painful blow, screamed a curse at her as he lunged forward, grabbed her ankles, and pulled her down.

Momentarily, oxygen again flowed into Myinga's lungs, and another scream began to escape from her lips when Singing Bird again grabbed her throat, hanging on tightly. "Maybe you will not be so lucky to visit our village and stay in our wigwams."

Myinga dug her nails into his wrists and fought to free herself, but Singing Bird's grip was strong, and he didn't seem to notice the pain her fingernails inflicted.

"Maybe your whisper was right, my beautiful but foolish woman," the first man said as he climbed on top of her, his weight holding her down.

Myinga heard him, but her fingernails were losing their deep grip on the wrists of Singing Bird. Darkness was closing in from the outside of her vision as she looked into the face of her captor as he continued.

"Maybe I am your destiny."

CHAPTER 17

Little Fawn dropped her head against Muckwa and snuggled in to him. "I'm so tired, Muckwa," she told her brown, fluffy dog named Bear. "I'll just doze for a while until Onadesh arrives."

As Little Fawn relaxed and drifted away, her thoughts were of the first night that Onadesh had officially courted her.

"Grandmother, he is playing his flute outside of our wigwam," she had whispered one evening.

The old woman nodded. "Do not go to him right away. Let him play a while. Come, let's have dinner."

"Should I at least acknowledge him?" Little Fawn had asked.

"No. We will prepare dinner."

Little Fawn glanced towards the doorway to the wigwam but obeyed her grandmother.

Four hours later, the old woman nodded again. "If you love him, it is time for you to go accept him."

Little Fawn felt butterflies in her stomach as she clapped her hands together. "What should I do?"

The old woman lifted a few green leaves in one hand and a bowl of crushed root in the other. "You must make him tea."

"Tea?"

"Not any tea. This is a tea made with ginseng root and the leaf of the monarda plant."

Little Fawn wrinkled up her nose. "Tea from bee balm? How about a regular mint?"

Her grandmother shook her head with a wise expression on her face. "This is our tea for love."

"Grandmother, he's been playing his flute outside of our wigwam for four hours. I think he's already in love."

"It is not love that he feels," she smiled wisely. "It is only a passing fancy."

Little Fawn felt her heart sink a little. "So this tea will make him love me?"

"In a way. It indicates that you accept his love. Come, we will make it together."

Minutes later, Little Fawn took the steaming cup of tea out

to Onadesh, whose flute playing stopped when she approached.

"Little Fawn, I have come to ask you to join me."

"In marriage?" she asked, feeling skeptical of his feelings after what her grandmother had told her.

"Yes. Will you move into my wigwam?" When Little Fawn hesitated, he continued, indicating to a sack next to him. "I have brought you many hooves for your jingle dress. You know I am a good provider."

"Yes, I know you are a mighty hunter." Little Fawn looked down at the cup in her hands before holding it out in offering to Onadesh. "My grandmother says you must drink this."

He smiled as if knew he had won her and took a sip, keeping his eyes on her. "Some kind of mint," he acknowledged as his focus looked at the cup.

Little Fawn looked back to the door of her wigwam where her grandmother made a gesture to her.

"You must finish the tea, and then you will have my answer," she told him.

"If that is the condition, I will drink it quickly." Onadesh tilted his head back and swallowed the entire cup of tea. His eyes seemed to have difficulty focusing for a moment until he let out a loud burp.

Little Fawn giggled. "How do you feel?"

He looked around before focusing on her again. "I feel like I just drank a lot of tea."

"How do you feel about me?" she giggled.

His eyes focused in on hers. "I – I feel so – " he searched for the words. "I feel that I must be with you."

"But why do you want me to move into your wigwam?"

He smiled an unusually warm smile. "Because you are meant to be with me."

"For how long?" she asked, still feeling unsure.

He reached for her hands. "Until there is no more."

Her eyes searched his for a moment before she smiled. "Yes."

"Yes?"

"Yes, I will go to your wigwam after our marriage feast."

Little Fawn's grandmother stepped out with a smile on her face and held up a blanket. "Take this," she said as she wrapped the blanket around the young couple. "Take this for your new home and go celebrate."

Little Fawn looked at her grandmother with surprise in her eyes.

Understanding her confusion, her grandmother continued. "Do not go to his wigwam, but go celebrate your love." She smiled at her granddaughter with a twinkle in her eyes.

Little Fawn smiled back at her grandmother before turning to Onadesh and lifting her shoulders in playful agreement. "We must find a place to celebrate."

Onadesh's eyes wandered for a moment before returning to hers with an excited air. "I know just the place."

Now Little Fawn smiled to herself in her sleep as she remembered that night. Muckwa let out a quiet growl, and she groggily awoke and looked around her. Screams in the forest intermingled with war whoops caused her to wake up quickly. Her senses scampered to get their bearings.

"What is happening, Muckwa?" she whispered to her companion.

Before Little Fawn could do anything, hundreds of Muscodesh people were running towards her through the dusk from the forest. Little Fawn froze in terror as she saw Odawa warriors throwing tomahawks into their backs, causing what seemed like every other Muscodesh to fall.

Starting to rise to her feet next to Muckwa, she whispered, "We must get out of the ravine, Muckwa."

Things happened quickly. Before Little Fawn could slip out a side of the ravine, hundreds of people were herded in around her like cattle with wolves guarding the opening to the narrow ravine.

Her hand dug into Muckwa's thick fur and grasped it. Screams surrounded her as the wolves closed in on the cattle and, one by one, began to annihilate them. Arrows and spears flew in, striking those around her.

Looking from one side to the other for a way out, Little Fawn turned to her left. Her eyes scanning the crowds for an escape, she finally saw someone looking at her from a long distance away. As she recognized him, her eyes softened, the fear leaving them, but she only saw shock and terror in the eyes of the other. She began to smile in recognition when she felt an arrow pierce and pass through the right upper side of her chest.

Her eyes slowly left those of the shooter and looked down at the feathered tail of the arrow jutting from her chest. Not believing what had happened, she looked back up to meet the eyes of the shooter.

"Wa-wash-ay-wesh Koons!" he screamed out her name in his native tongue, his voice carrying over the madness around her.

Little Fawn's eyes filled with shock and sorrow as she realized what had happened. She fell limply to the ground, and the chaos around her closed in.

CHAPTER 18

"I've arrived. Let the party start," Judy announced as she walked into the cupcake shop to report for work.

"Hi, Aunt Judy," Kylie called from behind her laptop in her office.

Judy smiled when she spotted Cupcake through the office window that separated it from the rest of the shop. "I'm telling you, Half Cake, you're getting too big to be on that desk."

Kylie's right hand left the keyboard of her laptop and stroked the black head of the pit-mix puppy. "Don't listen to her, Cuppie. We'll just get a bigger desk if that happens."

Cupcake's eyes were filled with adoration as she looked up at her owner.

"And a bigger shop," Judy mumbled before turning to the stainless steel island in the center of the shop. "So what's the cupcake du jour, Kylie? I hope you have a shorter name than yesterday."

"It's a sangria cupcake," Kylie called, leaning on her left hand as she continued to read the computer screen.

"Sangria cupcake? Only two words?" Judy put her hands on her hips as she stared at the cupcakes with the unassuming name. "That's a big improvement."

Kylie kept reading, ignoring her aunt.

"There are two kinds out here. What's the other?"

Kylie didn't respond, caught up in what she was reading.

"Hello, Earth to Kylie," her aunt called.

"Huh?"

"What's the second cupcake flavor?"

"Oh, just an experimental flavor," Kylie waved her hand dismissively.

"Well, people are going to want to know what it is," Judy told her.

Kylie's eyes left the screen for a moment as she thought. Turning to her aunt, she said, "How about a mint energy cupcake?"

Judy's face cringed. "Kylie Sue, how many times have I told you that health food doesn't belong in a cupcake shop?"

Kylie couldn't help but let a small smile slip out. "It's got eggs and butter in it, Aunt Judy. It's not that healthy."

"So where does the energy come from?"

"It's got a dose of ginseng in it."

Judy frowned and shook her head dismissively. "It's healthy, Kylie. No one will want it."

Letting a full, dimpled grin slip out, Kylie responded, "Well, why don't you try one. If you hate it, I'll drop them off at the fire station and not sell them."

Judy shrugged as she picked up a cupcake and inspected it. "I guess firemen need healthy treats," she mumbled to herself as she peeled the paper wrapping away and took a bite of the green cupcake with white frosting.

Kylie and Cupcake watched Judy closely as she slowly chewed and swallowed. Her eyes looked up for a moment as she thought and then took another bite.

"It's very clean tasting," she described it.

"And...?"

Judy thought a moment. "It's got a little zing to it." She made some sucking sounds with her mouth as she absorbed the flavor. "The mint tastes a little," her hand made small, slow circles in the air as her mind searched for the descriptor, "woody."

Kylie grinned at her. "So is it good enough to sell?"

Judy took another bite. "Yeah, I guess. I don't know if I'd make it again, but it's worth a shot."

"Thanks, Aunt Judy," Kylie said as she stood from the laptop.

"I might need to wash it down with a sangria cupcake for my cocktail hour today," Judy teased.

Kylie grabbed her purse, and Cupcake jumped off of the desk.

"So are you off to meet your hunky firefighter?" Aunt Judy asked, frosting on her upper lip as she chewed her third bite.

"Nope. He's fishing. It's just us girls today," she answered, bending to hook Cupcake's pink leash to her pink collar.

"Another swimming lesson?" Judy asked, popping the last of the cupcake into her mouth and licking her fingertips.

A full, dimpled grin emerging again on her face, Kylie answered, "No. We're going to hike the ravine at Devil's Elbow."

Judy's sated look vanished and was replaced by an unpleasant expression. "Why would you ever want to do that?" She shoved her thick glasses up her nose, and the top of the frame touched the heavy bangs of her gray-streaked bob.

"There's just got to be a reason we found that jingle dancer there, and I intend to figure it out."

"You really should take Jason with you," Judy told her with the shake of an index finger.

Kylie let out a sigh of disapproval. "Aunt Judy, I'm a big girl. I can take care of myself."

"Well, I'd just feel better if you weren't alone."

"I won't be. I have Cupcake with me," Kylie pushed the back door open and stepped out of the shop. "Have a great day, Aunt Judy," she called in a singsong tone as she walked away.

Judy let out a grunt and picked up another mint energy cupcake. "She sure was cheerful," she mumbled to herself as she peeled off another wrapper.

Kylie's white SUV, distinguished by the large cupcake magnets on each front door that read "Kylie Kakes," hugged the curves as she carefully navigated the Tunnel of Trees north of Harbor Springs. To her left was a cliff that dropped hundreds of feet to the beach of Lake Michigan. To her right were both cabins and mansions with incredible views that went over Lake Michigan to land on Beaver Island on a clear day.

"Wouldn't it be great to have a house out here, Cuppie?" Kylie asked the puppy that sat tall in the front seat to look through the windshield. "You have to sell a lot of cupcakes to afford these houses though," she informed her companion.

Cupcake let out a loud yawn without taking her eyes off of the curving road.

"Okay, here we are," she told the puppy as she pulled her SUV off the road next to the sign located in the center of the sharp turn.

Kylie kicked off her flip-flops and pulled on her hiking boots.

Holding Cupcake's leash, she led the puppy up to the large sign.

"Devil's Elbow," she read aloud. "A flowing spring in this ravine was believed by Indian tribes to be the home of an evil spirit who haunted the locality during the hours of darkness."

Cupcake looked up at the sign as if reading along and then looked at her owner when she stopped speaking.

"Fortunately," Kylie told the puppy, "we're not here during the hours of darkness."

Cupcake continued to look at her owner expectantly.

"So let's find this flowing spring."

Cupcake let out a yip, and Kylie stepped behind the sign and into the densely wooded and dark ravine.

CHAPTER 19

As Little Fawn lay on the ground in shock, blood running freely from the wound in the right side of her chest, Muckwa licked her face.

She reached a hand up to pet the head of the fluffy dog as the melee raged on around her. "Muckwa, you must run. Go, get out!" she told the dog, gesturing with her free arm.

Instead of obeying, Muckwa laid down by her side and licked the face of his owner.

"Muckwa Koons," she said more weakly, calling him Little Bear, "you must go. I cannot, but you can."

Muckwa scooted away from her and let out a yip.

"Go!"

Muckwa yipped again.

Little Fawn refocused on the arrow through her. Her hands moved to it and tried to pull it out, but the copper arrowhead caught in her back. She let out a yell of pain and frustration.

Muckwa scooted back and again yipped.

"Go!" she screamed at the dog. "Go and save your life!"

Arrows flew through the air above her, and members of the Muscodesh tribe fell lifeless as the massacre continued.

Muckwa yipped again.

Little Fawn picked up a stone with her left hand and hurled it at the large, fluffy dog. "Go!"

Instead of obeying, Muckwa approached his owner, grasped the shoulder corner of her dress in his mouth, and gave a hard tug.

"Go! I said, 'Go!'" she yelled again, wanting the dog to save its own life.

Muckwa gave the clothing a stronger tug this time and instead began to pull his owner.

"Muckwa, I cannot walk," Little Fawn choked as she looked down at her jingle dress. It was a dress for healing, but she could not heal herself now as the pool of her blood enlarged to encircle her head.

As if he understood, Muckwa grabbed a larger portion of his owner's dress and dragged her the few yards behind the pool and through the underbrush to the wall of the ravine.

"Muckwa, please go," she said weakly. "Leave me to die."

Muckwa let out another yip. He ran a few feet into the underbrush and then came back.

Little Fawn's eyes were closing now, and she no longer heard the screams of terror around her. "Go, Muckwa Koons," she said again. "Go."

Muckwa came forward again and took a large portion of her dress in his mouth. Slowly, the dog dragged her body through the underbrush, behind the pool, and through a very low opening in the side of the cliff.

Opening her eyes, Little Fawn looked around the tiny cave that had a small spring coming out of the back that ran past her and to the small pond outside. "You have brought me to safety," she said weakly to Muckwa, who stood over her. Her left hand tried to reach up to the large dog but fell short.

Muckwa lay down next to it and lay his head on it.

"Onadesh will find us, Muckwa. He promised," Little Fawn

said as her hand dropped weakly into the water that flowed past her. "He will find me and get the Midewiwin to heal me." She smiled weakly at the dog she loved so much. "I am a jingle dress dancer. I am chosen. I am special," she muttered to herself as more blood drained from her body and she grew weaker. "I know The Great Creator would not let me die like this. I am chosen," she repeated weakly. As the minutes turned into an hour, Little Fawn's eyes rolled back into her head, and she touched Muckwa's large, brown paw one last time as she realized her prophetic dream had come true. "I know Onadesh will not rest until he finds me, and I will not rest until I am found," were her final whispered words.

CHAPTER 20

Judy was licking the minty frosting of the second cupcake

from her fingers when she heard the front door of the shop jingle.

Turning, she saw Sam enter.

"What's up, Buttercup?" he asked cheerfully.

With an uncharacteristic smile, Judy stepped to the front

counter. "Well, aren't you looking handsome today, Sam Shepard,"

she complimented.

Sam squinted his eyes at her suspiciously. "Thanks, Sugar

Pea. I thought I'd stop by and see how your day was going."

Judy leaned onto the front counter and traced a pattern

onto the glass with her fingertip. "It's going well," she looked up at

him, "but, then again, I just got here."

Sam continued to look at her with caution. "Aren't you

going to tell me that I should only be here if I intend to buy

cupcakes? Lots of cupcakes?" he asked skeptically.

Judy smiled a drunken smile and waved her hand

dismissively at him. "Cupcake-schmupcake," she replied. "You don't need a reason to come see me, Sam."

"I don't?"

"No," she waved again before looking down to retrace her pattern on the glass display case. "As a matter of fact, I was hoping you'd want to go with me to Music In The Streets tonight."

Sam's eyes darted to the side before moving back to her. "You're asking me to do something with you?"

Judy bent from her hips enticingly as she arched her back and put the weight of her upper body on the display case. "Well, if you want to."

"I thought you didn't like me."

"Why would you say that?" she asked, looking up at him genuinely surprised.

His eyes darted to the side suspiciously and back again before answering, "Because you tell me that all the time."

She gently shook her head. "I like you just fine." Sam continued to look at her skeptically before she continued. "Okay, maybe I was playing hard to get," she hesitated and added a small shrug of her shoulders, "a little."

"So you really want me to go with you tonight?"

"Of course I do."

Seizing the moment, he pushed his luck. "Will you let me walk next to you instead of five feet behind you?"

"Of course."

"Will you introduce me to your friends?"

"Of course."

"Will you let me hold your – "

"Let's not get crazy," she held up a finger to interrupt.

Sam relaxed and placed his hand on top of hers to stop it from tracing its pattern on the display case. "Now, that's the Judy I know and love."

The door jingled behind him, and Jason walked in. His eyes moved from their faces to Sam's hand on Judy's, and he smiled, shaking his head in disbelief before asking, "Is Kylie around?"

Sobering, Judy looked at the handsome fire chief in his navy blue T-shirt and Dickies. "No, she's done for the day." She looked at Sam and continued conspiratorially, "That's the upside of coming in to work at five a.m."

Sam smiled.

"Okay," Jason acknowledged, watching the two older people closely. "Is she at the beach?"

"Nope," Judy replied, staring adoringly at Sam, who was squirming.

Realizing he was interrupting something, Jason cut to the chase. "So where can I find her?"

Judy's eyes rolled up, indicating her disapproval. "She went to Devil's Elbow."

Jason's smile vanished. "What for?"

"Didn't say."

"And you just let her?"

Sobering further, Judy slapped her heavy thighs and held her hands up questioningly. "What did you want me to do, tackle her? She's a grown woman, she can do what she wants."

"Call me. You should have called me," Jason said as he

turned and left the shop, his voice heavy with worry as he quickly

dismissed the flirtation that was going on before him.

"I'd better offer him my assistance," Sam said, pulling away

from his paramour.

"You're leaving?"

He smiled reassuringly. "Just for a while, my loverly," he

said playfully.

Judy looked worried. "Well, be careful."

Sam puckered his lips, sending her an air kiss before turning

to follow the fire chief out the front door of the shop.

"My goodness," Judy said to herself, regaining her senses

and pressing a palm to her chest, "what was that all about?"

Rubbing her sweaty palms on her pants, she turned to view

the work area of the shop and spotted Kylie's laptop still lit up in

the office. "She's always leaving that thing on," Judy muttered to

herself as she stepped across the shop and into the office, scooping

another mint energy cupcake off of the island on the way. "These

things are addicting," she said, the tip of her tongue lapping up some frosting. Seeing a photograph of two Native Americans on the screen with writing below it, she slipped into the seat and began to read.

Mumbling the story aloud to herself, she read, "In the Indian culture, when a young man fell in love with a woman, he went through certain procedures." Interested, she continued. "First, he would go to her father with gifts. If the father approved of the young man and consented to give his daughter to him, the young man would start his courtship." She looked at the cupcake before taking a bite. "Kylie and her love stories," she mumbled before looking back to the screen and continuing out of curiosity. "He would use his flute to play courting songs while the woman was inside her wigwam. Often, this would go on all night. Each brave had his own song that he would play for a woman, and it was usually a special song played only for her." Judy let out a sigh and muttered, "Blah, blah, blah," before wiping some frosting from the corner of her mouth and continuing. "If the woman liked the young man, she would prepare a special blend of tea. We call this blend the Indian Love Tea. She would then come out of her wigwam to the sound of the music and offer the young brave a cup of tea, a sign of mutual admiration."

"Huh," Judy said aloud. "I wonder what this has to do with Devil's Elbow?"

She scrolled down the page to where it listed the ingredients. "Sweet leaf, ginseng root, muira puama," she read the first three ingredients.

Her eyes moved uneasily to the kitchen island covered with both sangria cupcakes and mint energy cupcakes. Pursing her lips, she did a Google search. "Sweet leaf is monarda, a member of the mint family," she mumbled to herself as she stole another sideways glance at the cupcakes on the island countertop. Out of curiosity, she Googled muira puama and pushed the rolling chair away from the desk when the result popped up. "An aphrodisiac!" Color flooded into her full cheeks as she realized what had happened. "Kylie Sue!" she screamed loud enough to be heard at the boat docks.

CHAPTER 21

Onadesh stood frozen in position the second after he had released his bow. Had that been Little Fawn? Why would she be in the ravine with the Muscodesh? He looked around him with tired eyes. Was this their ravine? He'd thought they were in the ravine further to the south and Little Fawn was safe in their special place.

He hadn't slept for two days and was exhausted. He must have mistaken the ravines. Why else would Little Fawn be there? His mind was moving a million thoughts through it per second, but his body could not move from its position.

"What is wrong with you?" Nakoma asked his friend. "Keep shooting the arrows, or we will be here all night."

Onadesh still didn't move. His eyes looked at the spot where he thought he'd seen her, but she wasn't there now.

"I think I just shot my wife," he said, still holding the position he'd held when the fatal arrow had been released.

"You don't have a wife," Nakoma dismissed.

He was silent for a moment. "I was going to have her as

soon as this was over."

Nakoma looked at his friend. "You were going to marry a Muscodesh?"

Still looking through the viewer, he gave his head a slight shake. "No. She was Odawa."

Nakoma released another arrow into the ravine and watched another member of the Muscodesh tribe fall to the ground. "There are no Odawa in the ravine. They are Muscodesh that ran from the village."

Shaking his head harder, Onadesh said, "I know I saw her."

"Why would she be here?"

Onadesh felt his stomach turn as he finally lowered the bow and leaned over to vomit. Taking a deep breath of recovery, he said, "Because I told her to be here."

Nakoma looked at his friend with an uncomprehending expression on his face.

Recovering, Onadesh dropped the bow and, without saying another word to his friend, ran. He ran through the blood-thirsty warriors wielding their war clubs and tomahawks, through the barrage of arrows that were landing all around, and through the few remaining members of the Muscodesh tribe. He didn't look at the terror on their faces because he had terror on his own face as he ran with speed and agility over bodies, pushing the survivors out of his way. "Wa-wash-ay-wesh Koons!" he screamed as he ran. "Wa-wash-ay-wesh Koons!"

Growing more frantic as the realization of what he had done set in, he started turning over bodies in search of his beloved. "Wa-wash-ay-wesh Koons!" he called to each female corpse that he turned over, only to see that it wasn't Little Fawn.

As the last Muscodesh body in the ravine fell to the ground, Onadesh continued to examine corpses, determined to find Little Fawn.

When a hand landed softly on his shoulder, he turned sharply and drew his knife.

Nakoma held up both hands in surrender. "Onadesh, it is me."

Recognizing his friend, he placed a hand on each of his Nakoma's shoulders and shook him with urgency. "Help me find her."

Nakoma looked around at the carnage. "She is not here, Onadesh. These are Muscodesh."

"She is here," Onadesh argued with urgency. "I saw her eyes. They met mine."

Nakoma shook his head. "You are tired, my friend. You have fought valiantly, and you are exhausted and imagining things."

"No, I know I did not imagine it." He shook his friend again. "Help me look for her," his eyes pleaded, "please."

Nakoma looked around and finally nodded his head in agreement.

Lit only by the light from the full moon on a clear night, the two warriors turned over body after body in search of Little Fawn, but she was nowhere to be found.

"Onadesh, we must stop."

"No."

"She is not here."

"I saw her," he said with less conviction than before. "I saw her."

"No. She is not here," Nakoma repeated. "Maybe she heard the Muscodesh approaching and fled before we cornered them here."

Onadesh paused as he mulled over the possibility.

"She is probably back at the village and worrying about you," Nakoma offered.

Onadesh looked over the massacred corpses around him. "But I saw her," he told his friend weakly. His eyes met Nakoma's, and they had tears in them. "I saw her as I released my arrow to her."

Nakoma shook his head sadly. "You are tired, my friend. Very tired." He indicated to the bodies around him. "We have looked at them all, and she is not here."

Onadesh shook his friend's shoulders again. "I know what I saw, Nakoma. I know I saw her here." The tears broke free. "I know I shot her with my arrow."

Nakoma held his hands up. "Then where is she? I know she is a chosen jingle dress dancer, but jingle dress dancers do not disappear when they are shot with an arrow."

Onadesh looked even more panicked.

Nakoma slapped Onadesh's arm. "Come. Let's go back to the village. I am sure she awaits you there."

"No," Onadesh said, bending to turn another corpse to view its face.

"Come," his fiend pulled harder at Onadesh's arm.

Onadesh stood and looked into the ravine lit by moonlight. His chest heaving, he screamed, "Wa-wash-ay-wesh Koons!" with every ounce of strength in his body before collapsing to the ground.

CHAPTER 22

Kylie hiked through the base of the ravine, Cupcake safely secured on her leash next to her owner. The area was eerily quiet, and Kylie jumped when a hawk flew overhead and squawked.

She shivered as she remembered Aaron's words, "We were told to stay away from Devil's Elbow."

"Why?" Kylie had asked.

"They would not tell us, and we did not ask," was Aaron's reply.

The trees were thick, and the light was sparse as Kylie hiked through the dense forest.

"How do you feel, Cupcake?" she asked the puppy, trying to lighten the mood. "Is it just me, or is it slightly creepy back here?"

Cupcake walked just in front of her owner, uncharacteristically quiet.

"I'll bet that spring is hundreds of years old and is all dried up now," Kylie said aloud as she looked from side to side with wide eyes. "I mean, it's just a story by – "

She was interrupted by Cupcake's low growl and realized the puppy had stopped walking. Her eyes followed the dog's gaze and saw ahead of them a spotted fawn similar to the one she had seen at the beach.

"Cupcake, don't even think about it."

Cupcake growled again and lunged forward, pulling Kylie behind her.

"Cupcake Marie, stop! Bad girl!" she called.

The fawn ran ahead of them, and Cupcake followed, using her forty-five pounds of sheer muscle to pull her owner along.

Jumping over fallen trees and blazing through underbrush that tore at her clothing Kylie did her best to keep up. The three traveled over gullies, around stumps, and deeper and deeper into the ravine.

"Cupcake, baaaaaad girl! Baaaaaad!" she scolded the dog between gasps for air.

The fawn leaped effortlessly over a large fallen log, and Cupcake followed. Kylie thrust one leg out in front, forming a split leap in the air that only a trained ballerina should attempt. As she followed the puppy through the air, she came down on the side of her foot. Unstable, it rolled onto her ankle, and Kylie released the leash as she cried out in pain.

As if sensing that Kylie had fallen, the fawn turned and stopped. Cupcake stood growling at it, all the hair on her back standing on end.

"Cupcake, that was very bad," Kylie scolded through tears as she fought to breathe through the pain of the twisted ankle.

Minutes passed, and the pain finally eased enough for Kylie to open her eyes. In front of her was a small pond, similar to the one in the lower ravine only muddier. Behind some large boulders surrounding the pond stood the fawn. On the other side stood Cupcake growling at the fawn.

"Cupcake, it's just a baby like you. Leave it alone."

Cupcake didn't budge.

Assured that the fawn could outrun Cupcake if it had to, Kylie looked around the dark forest before looking back at the small, muddy pond. "So that's the spring that the evil spirits come out of when darkness sets in?" she asked no one in particular. "Pfft," she made the sound with her mouth. "Doesn't look so scary to me."

The hawk circling above let out a loud screech, and Kylie tried to see it through the trees.

"I guess I'd better try to get to some ice for this," she commented, placing her injured leg out straight in front of her and pushing herself up on the log. Cupcake and the fawn didn't move.

"Cupcake, come," she commanded.

Cupcake ignored the order.

"Cupcake Marie Branson, come," Kylie called again.

Cupcake's eyes never left the fawn.

Kylie rose to her full height, holding the injured foot out in front of her. "Ooh, you are so way not getting any treats for – for – " she struggled to think of an appropriate punishment, "at least a week."

Hopping towards the loose leash behind the puppy, she

grabbed a large stick to use as a cane to help balance herself. Reaching the leash, she bent to scoop it up. "Bad girl. Baaaaaad girl," she scolded again before giving the leash a tug to get the puppy to turn and leave.

Cupcake resisted, and it was the straw that broke the camel's back. Tears of pain and frustration escaped Kylie's eyes when she realized she wouldn't have the strength to pull the puppy away balanced only one foot.

"Cupcake, come," she commanded, giving the leash a tug.

Cupcake wouldn't move.

Tears running down her cheeks, Kylie turned and attempted to pull the puppy with her.

Cupcake let out a yip and resisted.

"Cupcake, please," she pleaded as the fawn watched them, not leaving her spot by the pool of water that had once been large enough to carve the ravine they stood in.

Kylie pulled out her cell phone and swiped the screen to view it. "Shhh – ugar," she cursed to herself, "I have no bars." She held the phone up in all directions before giving up and slipping it back into the pocket of her pants. "Tugging on the leash now looped over her wrist, she took a couple hops and felt Cupcake resist again. "This is going to take all day," she muttered to herself.

The bird above her screeched again, and she realized with a shiver that "all day" would take her into the hours of darkness the sign had warned of.

CHAPTER 23

Onadesh threw open the flap of deer hide that served as a door to the wigwam. "Is Little Fawn here?" he asked without announcing himself to the old woman.

Looking both surprised and confused, the grandmother with long, white braids shook her head. "No. She left the night that you left for battle."

"Where did she go?"

The old woman shrugged. "She did not tell me. I did not even know she was leaving. She just disappeared after the war council."

Onadesh's empty eyes looked around, not yet ready to comprehend reality. "Where could she be?"

The woman looked pointedly at Onadesh. "With you."

The empty eyes filled with sorrow. "She is not with me." He looked around. "Where is Ojig? He will know."

"Otter is with his friends near the lakeshore, but he has not seen her either."

Onadesh shook his head. "That is not possible. He will know." Without farewell, he ducked out of the wigwam as quickly as he had entered. He ran from the village and the short distance through the forest to the beach where he saw three boys skipping stones into the water. "Ojig, where is Little Fawn?"

Ojig looked confused. "She went to meet you."

Onadesh placed his hands on the boy's shoulders and shook him. "Where? Where was she going to meet me?"

Ojig looked confused. "She said it was your place." His eyes darted momentarily to his friends and then back to the man who was his future brother-in-law. "Your secret place," he whispered.

"I cannot find her there." Onadesh remained low to look into the boy's eyes. "Where else would she be?"

Ojig held out his hands. "I have not seen her since she left after the war council."

Onadesh felt his heart sink. "No," he pushed the boy away from him harder than he meant to, "she is here. I know she is here."

He turned and ran back towards the village as Ojig watched him with a stunned expression.

"Where else would she be, Onadesh?" the boy called after the warrior.

Onadesh didn't reply as he tore through the forest and back to the village.

"What has happened to my sister?" Ojig whispered.

Onadesh ran from wigwam to wigwam in the large village, searching and calling for Little Fawn. When he exhausted that option, he ran to the marshes of wild rice and the fields of squash, beans, and corn in search of Little Fawn, but his search was futile. Out of desperation, he ran the trail to their secret place that was now littered with bodies. "Little Fawn!" he called her name over and over until his voice failed him. He ran along the lakeshore and then climbed the bluff in search of her. "Little Fawn!" he called with a hoarse voice again and again until he bent over and dropped his hands to his knees and the sobs of regret, desperation, and utter sorrow broke loose from his lungs. "What have I done? Where are you, Little Fawn?"

The next night, Onadesh sat like an empty shell staring into the council fire as the men spoke around him. All he saw were the orange flames dancing hypnotically in front of him. His feet were bloody and raw from his extensive search. His body was battered from battle, and his soul seemed to have left his body as he stared ahead, feeling empty inside.

Aneamishi sat weakly to his left, a large compress strapped onto his shoulder wound by the Midewiwin. Nakoma sat to the right of Onadesh, solemn and listening to the elder members of the tribe.

"Already the stench of dead bodies drifts towards our village," said an elder.

"The battle came too close. You put your people in danger," another elder scolded.

The warriors sat quietly and listened as the comments continued.

"Already the wolves come from the forest to feed on the

bodies that lay by the hundreds." The old man held out an arm and gestured towards the people of the village. "Our children are not safe outside of the village with so many wolves nearby."

"The bodies must be buried," Chief Sagima said solemnly.

"We cannot dig graves for hundreds of people," Nakoma protested. "We have already fought valiantly and done your bidding. We are tired and need to rest. We cannot dig hundreds of graves."

Onadesh still stared into the fire, seemingly oblivious to the conversation around him.

"Nakoma is right," the first elder agreed. "Our warriors are battered and weak from fighting both the Sioux and the Muscodesh. They cannot dig hundreds of graves."

"We cannot leave the bodies out to decay," the chief said. "The stench will cause us to move the village before winter if we leave it as it is. The wolves will make the forest unsafe for not only children but anyone traveling alone." He looked at the group solemnly. "The bodies must be buried."

"Then let us only create one grave," said a man as he stood to speak from the outskirts of the circle.

"It is still much to dig," Nakoma argued. "It would be a massive hole."

"No," said the man on the outskirts of the firelight. "We would not have to dig at all." He drew a deep breath and turned to face the people around him. "Let us move all of the bodies to the back of the ravine. We will stack them and build a wall to hold them in their grave."

"That will not stop the stench or the wolves," the chief commented.

Unfinished with his plan, the man continued. "Once the wall is built and the bodies are secured, men will climb to the top of the bluff. They will break off large portions from the top, causing the dirt to fall onto the bodies and bury them."

Silence came over the group as they thought the idea over. The only sounds were the crackling of the fire and a faint drum.

"It will affect the small stream that runs through the ravine," the chief said.

"The water will no longer be safe to drink," said one man.

Another commented, "Or it may stop the water flow completely."

"It does not matter," said Nakoma, standing to make his point. "We have the big lake of fresh water right next to us. There are many other springs along the shoreline. This one will not be missed."

The Midewiwin stood and spoke for the first time. "If we do this, we must be sure no one will drink this water again." He looked around the group with an expression that was both sad and serious. "We must somehow keep people away from it."

"How will we do that?" Nakoma asked from his spot in the circle.

The old Midewiwin sat silent in thought for a moment before continuing. "From this day forward, it will be said that evil spirits flow from the spring, for surely it will bring illness or death to anyone who drinks such contaminated water."

"It will be the evil spirits of the Muscodesh," said Nakoma coldly.

The council nodded in solemn agreement, and seconds of silence ticked by before Chief Sagima spoke.

"The Odawa have had their revenge. The Muscodesh have been wiped from the face of the Earth." He looked at the large group of people around him and continued. "As the men move the bodies, the women and children will gather every arrowhead, every tool, every last piece from the ravine that would let anyone know that the Muscodesh ever existed. The pieces will be placed with the bodies of the owners." He looked around at the group that listened to their leader. "When that is finished, their village will be burned." He looked again to the women. "As before, the women and children will gather every item left after the burning and ensure that it is destroyed."

The chief tapped his staff on the ground once before he continued. "There will be no stories told of the Muscodesh. They will be wiped from our history." His head moved slowly from one side of the ring to the other as he spoke, making eye contact with many. "Instead, the story will be of a spring from which flows an evil spirit during the hours of darkness. No man is to go there."

A quiet murmur ran through the crowd.

"We will begin tomorrow," Nakoma agreed. He looked at the crowd before continuing. "We have lost many men, but we will need one man on site to lead the project." He thumped his chest with his fist. "I can do it."

Before any of the elders could agree to assign the job, another voice spoke for the first time. "I will do it."

Both Nakoma and Aneamishi turned to look at their friend in astonishment.

Without looking away from the flames, his eyes glazed over, Onadesh repeated, "I will do it."

CHAPTER 24

Once Kylie pulled Cupcake away from the muddy spring and the fawn, her efforts to get back to her car did not progress as quickly as she hoped. One wrist through the looped handle on Cupcake's leash and the other holding a stick as a cane, she tried to take baby steps, keeping as much weight off of the painful ankle as possible.

"This really sucks," she muttered to Cupcake, who walked along next to her owner unusually quiet and not tugging on her leash.

A large stick snapped to her right in the dark ravine, and Kylie turned sharply in an attempt to see what caused the sound. "It's getting dark, and the trees are so dense here that I can't see very far," she told Cupcake. "I sure hope it was the fawn." She looked around nervously, but the fawn had disappeared into the forest as soon as she had turned to work her way back to the car.

She took a few more steps and heard a loud snap again in the same direction. Snapping her head to see what caused it, she saw nothing. Exhaling slowly, her eyes scanned the ridge of the ravine and then looked back. She inhaled quickly, unable to blink. On the ridge, looking down at her, stood a tall Native American. His body was covered with tattoos, and his head was shaved except for a thick tuft on the top that dropped to his shoulders.

Cupcake began to growl a low, soft growl.

Unable to speak, Kylie felt sweat begin to break out on her body as she looked at him. He was dressed in only a skirted loincloth and high moccasins. Kylie could see the taut muscles on his lean body as her eyes traveled up to his face. Her breath caught again when she saw his eyes looking hatefully into hers.

"Stay to the right, and I'll stay to the left!" she heard someone yell.

Unable to comprehend where the sound was coming from, she remained frozen, caught in the frighteningly hateful stare of the man on the other side of the ravine.

Flashlights broke through the darkness of the trees on the edges of the ravine and progressed towards her.

"Keep moving straight ahead. I'm not sure how far we'll have to follow this ravine!" some yelled.

Breaking her stare-induced trance, Kylie looked to her left and saw the flashlights and realized people were coming for her. Still unable to speak, she looked back to where the Native American had been watching her, but he was gone. Her eyes darted from side to side around her in the dim light, but she didn't see him.

Kylie felt a shudder run up her spine, and her stomach tightened as she felt like vomiting.

A light shone on her as she bent over, holding her cramped stomach.

"Kylie!"

She recognized Jason's voice, but she couldn't respond. Her eyes moved back to the ridge where her watcher had been. Terrified, she again scanned it with her eyes, searching for him.

"She's over here, guys!" she heard Jason call. Large sticks snapped in his wake as he made his way towards her.

"Kylie!" he called to her again.

Kylie still couldn't respond, and Cupcake didn't make a peep. The air suddenly felt heavy to her as her eyes continued to scan the ridge. Her shirt was wet with sweat, and Cupcake hadn't moved a step. She realized she was struggling to draw in a breath when strong arms wrapped around her, pulling her into their safe embrace but leaning her weight onto her twisted ankle.

"Aaaaah!" she let out a scream in pain.

"Kylie, what is it? Tell me what's wrong."

She felt tears flowing again and, for once, her pride was the last thing on her mind. "My ankle. You pushed my weight onto my ankle. I twisted it."

Without saying a word to chastise her, Chief Jason Lange easily scooped her into his arms to carry her down the ravine and back to safety.

"Mel, grab Cupcake's leash, will you?" he commanded when the other flashlight drew near.

"Got it," Mel told him as he bent to scoop up the leash from where Kylie had dropped it.

"Radio the team and call off the search."

Kylie didn't say anything as Jason carried her back through the ravine. Her eyes remained on the ridge where the terrifying man had been.

"We'll get you back, Kylie. Just hold tight. I know you're going to be okay," he lulled to her as he walked easily through the underbrush.

"There was a man," Kylie finally whispered fearfully when they were far enough away to lose sight of the ridge.

"A man?"

Kylie nodded and looked at Jason's face for the first time, seeing the concern written all over it.

"What did he say?"

"Nothing," she replied in a trance-like tone. "He was just watching me."

"That's weird."

"He was awful," she whispered. "Evil."

Jason paused his confident steps through the underbrush to

look at her. "You'll be okay, baby." He gently kissed her forehead. "You're just in shock. You'll be okay."

The closer they got to her car, the more Kylie regained her senses. "It's dark out?" She sounded surprised.

"Yes. You've been gone for over ten hours."

Kylie looked at him with confused eyes when she saw the fire truck with flashing lights and numerous other cars parked at the precarious bend in the road. "But it was just a short hike." Her eyes met his. "I was only gone an hour or so."

He looked straight ahead as he walked up to the firetruck. "Whatever you say." One of the guys pulled the door open for him, and he set her gently inside.

"Where's Cupcakie?" Kylie asked, looking beyond her rescuer.

Jason glanced over his shoulder to a flashlight moving towards them from the dark woods. "Mel's right behind us with her." He dropped to a knee and started to roll up her pants and remove a boot. "Now let's have a look at this ankle."

"Be gentle," Kylie begged as he tried to tug the boot off, causing her to draw in her breath sharply. "Undo the laces all the way."

Heeding her advice, he slipped off the boot and sock. Gently holding her foot, he palpated the area. "This is a serious injury, Kylie. I can't believe you even walked at all on it."

Kylie looked down at the swollen appendage. "It hurt so badly that I couldn't breathe at first."

Jason examined the ankle. "Did you roll it in or out?"

"Out."

"That would explain the purple along here," he gently pointed along the outside of her foot. He looked up at her. "I think you should go in for X-rays."

"X-rays? For a twisted ankle?"

"I think there's a good chance you chipped the bone. It's more common than you'd think with serious ankle injuries."

"Ooooh, no," Kylie leaned back and let out a low moan.

"Boss, did you call off the APB?" one of the firefighters

asked the chief.

"No," he looked at Kylie and gave her a small grin, "my hands were kind of full. Go ahead and do it."

For the first time, Kylie noticed just how many cars and people were at Devil's Elbow. "You put out an APB on me?"

"When you weren't in your car, we didn't know if you'd hiked up or down or been abducted."

"An APB?" she repeated, more alarmed.

The chief had a sheepish expression. "Maybe it was a bit overkill."

"A bit?" her emotions were swinging the opposite way from where they were when he'd first found her, and she momentarily forgot her fear. "Haven't we had a talk about this?"

"About APBs?"

"About rescuing me."

He pointed towards her ankle. "Kylie, it's not like you were going to be walking out of there by yourself in the dark."

"It wasn't that dark," she argued weakly. "How many times

have I told you there's no rescuing?"

"A lot," he acknowledged, hiding his irritation caused by her complete lack of gratitude.

"Jason, I'm not some sort of damsel in distress that needs you to always swoop in and save her. I know a lot of women get a charge out of that, but I can take care of myself."

Jason crossed his arms and looked at her without saying a word.

"We're supposed to be equals," she moved her hand to gesture between the two of them. "You don't see me going around rescuing you all the time, do you?"

He continued to silently watch her.

"No, you don't," she answered her own question. She felt her emotions escalating beyond her control as she transferred the intense fear she had felt staring into the hateful eyes of the man watching her. "And you certainly don't see me going around issuing APBs on you, do you?"

"You don't really have the authority for that," he said

calmly.

"But I'm just saying, if I did, I wouldn't be prancing around issuing them. Shoot, am I going to be on the news tonight? Does everyone in town know?" She slapped her palm to her forehead. "I can hear the headline now, Cupcake-maker turns into devil's food at Devil's Elbow."

The corners of Jason's mouth twitched as he forced himself to hold back a smile.

She removed her palm to look at him again. Her tone regained some of its sanity. "Seriously, you've really got to limit the rescuing."

"Ba-jeebers!" Sam exclaimed as he hobbled up to Kylie, his eyes focused on her injury. "Is that a knee or an ankle?"

Kylie paused her tirade to look at her injury again.

"I mean I've heard of cankles," Sam continued, "but that's more like a – a – " his eyes drifted up for a moment as he thought, " – a knee-kle."

"Sam, why don't you go make sure Cupcake has water,"

Jason offered a distraction.

Sam glanced around for the dog before looking back to Kylie and pointing a finger at her. "Listen, you're damn lucky this fella found you, young lady."

Kylie started to roll her eyes.

"Everyone knows strange things happen here after dark." He shook his head dismissively. "I don't know what you were thinking snooping around out here alone. Judy's going to be so upset."

Kylie blushed, embarrassed, and Sam turned to tend to Cupcake.

Avoiding eye contact with Jason, she ran her hands lightly over the swollen area, giving her temper moments of silence to calm. "I'm sure I'd hop out of here eventually," she mumbled quietly.

"So next time you just want me to go fishing and leave you in the middle of the woods at night?"

She shrugged, "Technically, you probably wouldn't go fishing at night."

"So you want me to leave you in the middle of the woods, injured, with some creepy guy walking around?"

She had momentarily forgotten about the man. Her eyes looked into the dark woods behind him, and she shuddered. "No, I don't want you to leave me out there with him," she whispered. She listened and heard the lake lapping against the shore behind and below her. In front of her, she heard nothing. Even if the bustle of the other people wasn't here, she realized she would hear nothing. Not even crickets. Her eyes softened and lowered to look at Jason as he knelt and held a bag of ice to her injury. Her hand slid down her leg and rested on his. "Thank you," she whispered to him, giving his hand a small squeeze.

CHAPTER 25

As the chief had commanded, Onadesh led his people to the ravine that had once been a special place to himself and Little Fawn. Leading the effort, he tirelessly pulled body after body to the back of the ravine, again checking each to be sure it was not Little Fawn. The stench was overwhelming, but he worked tirelessly, strapping a thin piece of buckskin over his nose to help filter the air.

"You know she is not here," Nakoma reminded his friend as he carried the feet of a body to which Onadesh held the hands.

"I know what I saw," Onadesh said stubbornly without looking up from the corpse.

"You saw what you wanted to see."

"I did not want to see Little Fawn struck by my arrow."

Nakoma let out a grunt as they lifted the body over a log. "Of course not. But you wanted to see Wa-wash-ay-wesh Koons. You were very tired. You imagined her."

The two men swung the body twice before releasing it onto the pile and turning their backs to look down the ravine that opened to the big lake.

"Then where is she, Nakoma?"

"Maybe she went back to Manitoulin Island. You said her dog is missing, too. Maybe she thought it would be safer there and left."

Onadesh shook his head. "She would not have disobeyed my wishes." He thought another moment as his eyes looked over the sea of bodies to the big lake. "She would not have left me," he whispered.

Nakoma slapped his friend on the back. "Then she is well. You will find her. Let us get this chore finished."

Nakoma stepped forward as Onadesh hesitated, staring into the distance.

"Onadesh! Onadesh!"

The warrior turned to the sound of his name.

"Onadesh, Muckwa has returned!" Ojig shouted as he approached the warrior.

"Muckwa? Just Muckwa?"

Ojig nodded as he placed his hands on his knees to catch his breath.

Onadesh bent to match his eye level to that of the breathless boy. "Little Fawn was not with him?"

"No," Ojig replied between gasps for air.

"Where is Muckwa now?"

Ojig lifted a hand to point. "At the wigwam with grandmother."

Onadesh looked at Nakoma.

"Go, my friend," Nakoma told him.

Onadesh gave Ojig a quick pat on the back before his strong legs pushed into a sprint, and he disappeared into the thick forest that surrounded the ravine.

CHAPTER 26

Kylie crossed the street in front of her cupcake shop to the library, swung open the door of the brick, two-story building, and began to climb the stairs. One hand gripped the railing as she limped in her walking cast. The scent of fudge from the shop on the first floor filled the stairwell, and she inhaled deeply and smiled as she reached the top.

"Hey, Mrs. Smith," Kylie greeted the librarian who sat behind the large desk in the center of the floor. Her short, gray curls remained perfectly in place as she looked over her glasses that were held on by a light chain.

"Well, if it isn't the cupcake queen herself."

Sam turned in the chair he sat in at the desk to face the newcomer. "Well, hello, young lady. How's the knee-kle?"

"Ha, ha," Kylie tolerated as she limped forward. "Much better, thank you."

"You're lucky you're not on crutches."

"What happened to your ankle?" Mrs. Smith asked,

removing her glasses and releasing them to hang on the chain around her neck.

"Oh, I twisted it in a fall and chipped part of a bone on the outside of my ankle," Kylie informed as she paused in front of the desk.

"So Jason was right about the chipped bone, huh?" Sam commented.

"Yes, he was right," Kylie sighed as she dropped into one of the cushioned armchairs next to the librarian's desk.

"All that running you do can be dangerous," Mrs. Smith commented. "You've got to keep your eyes on the sidewalk."

"Oh, she wasn't running," Sam jumped in. "She was nosing around out at Devil's Elbow."

Mrs. Smith threw Kylie an alarmed look.

"I wasn't nosing around," Kylie corrected.

"Oh, excuse me." Sam looked at Mrs. Smith. "Trespassing. She was trespassing out at Devil's Elbow and twisted her ankle."

"Why would anyone want to do that?" Mrs. Smith asked,

looking back to Kylie.

Kylie sighed and sunk deeper into the chair. "I just wanted to see what the spring looked like." Eager to change the subject, she looked at Sam. "I thought you were a retired librarian."

"I am."

"So why are you here?"

"I just come back to visit and make sure Greta here knows what she's doing," he replied, winking at the 70-plus-year-old librarian.

Kylie looked closely at the two for a few seconds. "So you have nothing else to do?"

Sam looked at his watch. "Well, I plan to go visit your aunt after this, but then I'm free until Bingo at seven o'clock tonight."

Kylie nodded in understanding. "Well, maybe you two can help me out with some information." She looked back and forth at the two librarians before continuing. "What can you tell me about Devil's Elbow that I can't find on Google or learn from Aaron?"

"What's Google?" Sam asked seriously.

"It's a way to search online," Mrs. Smith informed him simplistically.

Sam held up his hands in surrender. "I'm glad I got out of here while people still used the card catalog."

"Well, what do you know from books?"

"What did you find on Google?" Mrs. Smith countered.

"Very little," Kylie turned to the woman in the tan blazer with the conservative expression on her face. "Just that it's one of the most haunted places in Michigan, but no one seems to know for sure why."

Mrs. Smith pinched an arm of her glasses between two fingers as she thought. "I've heard of voices after dark."

"Yeah, I've heard that. I was looking for a reason why."

"The voices after dark is pretty common knowledge," Sam chirped in.

"So do you have any Native American books with information on it?" Kylie asked the two.

Mrs. Smith slowly shook her head thoughtfully. "None that I

can think of."

Kylie looked to Sam expectantly as he touched his lips together, making a light popping noise as he thought. Finally, he lifted a finger, and the popping stopped. "Not a Native American book, but I think I may have something to help you."

"What is it?"

Sam's eyes darted around the room as he struggled to remember a location. Pushing himself slowly out of the chair, he beckoned to her with his arm. "Let's go over here."

Kylie pushed herself up and limped after him down the aisles of bookshelves made of dark wood.

Sam slowed and ran a fingertip along the books until he stopped on one and pulled it out. "Ever hear of a fella by the name of Ivan Swift?"

Kylie slowly shook her head thoughtfully until she came up with an answer. "I've heard of Thorne Swift Nature Preserve."

Sam snapped his fingers and pointed at Kylie. "Same family."

"So who was Ivan Swift?"

Sam lifted his free hand and spread the fingers for emphasis as he spoke. "A local artist and poet that hit the big-time."

"Big-time?"

"He was very well known for his work." Sam opened the book and fanned through the pages as Kylie looked over his shoulder.

"You're looking in a poetry book?"

"Of sorts," he mumbled to himself as he scanned the pages before stopping.

Kylie squinted her eyes to read the page. "The Trail Road," she read the poem title softly.

Sam ran his finger slowly down the page before stopping. "Here now," he indicated, "this is the part that mentions Devil's Elbow." He handed the book to Kylie and stepped back.

Kylie searched for the spot for a moment. "The third and fourth stanzas?"

"Yup."

Kylie read aloud. "It winds across the mill-creek and up the Wasson Hill and, after earnest rainfalls, it has a wash to fill. A wall is laid to old walls, to hold the Hurdle Bend, and on the Devil's Elbow, the god of carts defend!"

Kylie looked up at Sam, her brows scrunched together as she fought to comprehend the poem. "What does it mean?"

The retired librarian smiled and shrugged his shoulders. "I guess that's for you to determine. Maybe, if you read the entire poem, it will make more sense."

Kylie let out a sigh, hobbled over to one of the study tables, and pulled out a chair. An hour later, she was still reading the book and scratching out notes when a hand landed on either side of her and a kiss brushed her cheek.

"Hi, Babe," Jason greeted her softly as he pressed his cheek to hers and focused on what she was reading. "What's up?"

"Oh, Sam gave me this book with this weird poem in it." She pointed her finger to the third stanza. "Does this make any sense to you?"

Jason mumbled the lines of the poem under his breath. "Nope," he told her as he gave her cheek another kiss in consolation.

"The part that bothers me is 'A wall is laid to old walls.'"

"What about it?"

"I don't remember seeing a wall out there."

"There was a lot of undergrowth. It could have been hidden."

She focused on the page and drummed her fingers. "I suppose so." He lingered, and she pushed the chair away so she could look at him. "What are you doing here anyway?"

"I went to your shop, and Judy said you might be up here."

She crossed her arms, getting ready to argue if he began to tell her she should have told him she was crossing the street. "So what's up?" she asked skeptically.

He grinned an impish grin, baring white teeth with a small space between the front two. "I wanted to know if you wanted to go on a date tonight."

"Say yes," Sam shouted from the desk where he and Mrs. Smith sat watching the two.

Kylie smiled. "A date to do what?"

"What everyone in this town does for a date."

"Well, I only grew up spending summers here, so you'll have to fill me in. What do people here do on a date?"

Still showing his teeth through a smile, he said, "Get an ice cream cone and walk the streets after dinner."

"In a non-prostitutional sense, I hope," she smirked, and his grin widened. "That's it?"

"And the docks."

"The docks?"

"To look at the boats."

Kylie smiled and nodded in understanding as she bit her bottom lip.

"So what do you say?"

"You had me at 'ice cream.'"

CHAPTER 27

"So I have something to show you," Jason said at the end of dinner, setting his wine glass down after taking the last full sip.

Kylie looked at him suspiciously. "This isn't a sex talk, is it?"

Jason looked momentarily startled before spitting some of the wine through his nose. "What? No. Why would you think that?" he asked, holding the white cloth napkin up to his dripping nose and upper lip.

Kylie's expression went from suspicious to embarrassed. "Well, I don't know. It's been two months, and I figured – "

"You figured I lacked enough class to broach the subject by telling you I wanted to show you something?"

Kylie bared her teeth in a mock smile and held up her hands as she shrugged. "So what did you want to show me?"

Jason threw her an irritated look as he reached into his back pocket and pulled out a piece of paper folded in half lengthwise.

As he held it out to her, Kylie looked at it with uncertainty. "What is it?"

"A coroner's report."

Her eyes lit up. "Ooh, really?" Then she remembered something, and her face fell. "What? I don't get to meet with him in person this time?"

"The body wasn't found on your property this time."

"Oh." She looked disappointed.

"I'm sure we could dig another one up at your house if we looked around long enough," he offered, still holding out the piece of paper.

She grinned and snatched it from him. Unfolding it, her eyes scanned down. "DNA says," she mumbled to herself as she scanned the document, "Native American female. Age undetermined. Remnants of whitetail cervus – must mean deer -- and canis."

She looked up to Jason. "Canis? Cannabis?" She held the document to the side and shook her head in question. "They found pot with her?"

Jason grinned his spaced grin. "'Canis' is the Latin word for dog."

"Ah," she relaxed a little. "Makes more sense than telling me she was a stoner."

Jason smirked and watched her look down to continue to read, but she didn't.

Staring at the paper for a moment, she looked up to Jason with sad eyes. "So her dog died with her?"

"Or maybe it was a wild dog, and he ate her carcass."

"Or attacked and killed her and dragged her back to its lair," Kylie shivered.

"No," Jason shook his head. "Keep reading."

Kylie looked back down at the paper, mumbling inaudibly until she got to the words, "'Copper arrowhead.'" She looked up to Jason with an incredulous expression. "So someone shot her with an arrow."

Jason nodded, a solemn expression on his face.

Kylie flipped to skim the second page as she said, "Were there two arrowheads? Maybe the dog got shot, too."

"Only one."

Kylie finished skimming the page before drumming her fingertips thoughtfully on the white linen tablecloth of the waterfront restaurant as Jason signed the bill.

"If the dog was eating her carcass, why would he die there if he wasn't shot?"

"Thank you," Jason said, handing the small, black folder to the waitress before turning his attention back to Kylie.

"It could have been there before her."

"Possibly," Kylie said, lost in thought.

"Are you ready for our ice cream walk?"

She grinned a dimpled grin as she rose from the table. "I saved room."

Jason held out his arm to allow her to pass by him in her white, linen tank dress paired with one flip-flop and her walking cast. Leaning in to her as his hand dropped to her waist, he whispered into her ear, "By the way, did I tell you that you look stunning tonight?"

She flashed her dimples at him again. "Actually, you did, but a girl can never hear it often enough."

His lips grazed her cheek in a soft kiss; and, minutes later, he was strolling, and she was easily limping down Main Street with ice cream cones in their hands.

"Are you sure you're okay to walk?" he asked protectively.

"Yeah. It's feeling better." She looked down at the walking cast that she unstrapped and took off at night. "I just can't wait to get this thing off for good."

"You're lucky you didn't hurt yourself worse," he commented. "You're sure you're okay to walk to the docks?"

"Yes," she dismissed him easily as she smiled and took in her surroundings. "You know what I like about this town?" she asked, licking dripping ice cream from her chin.

"Besides the fire chief?"

"Yeah, besides him," she commented, leaning to lick the dripping exterior of the cone. She waved her hand at the brightly-painted false-front buildings around her. "It's like stepping back in time."

"Sort of."

"I mean besides the cars."

"And firetrucks."

She grinned at him again and nudged him with her elbow. "I mean there's the old buildings, there's the history, and there are no fast-food restaurants."

"You're right about that," he agreed, chomping into his sugar cone.

"And it's quiet."

"That it is."

"And," she continued, gesturing to the corner in front of her, "there are little natural-spring water fountains just plopped throughout town randomly." She leaned over and took a sip before rinsing her sticky ice cream fingers in the water.

Jason popped the rest of the cone into his mouth and followed her lead, rinsing his fingers in the water.

"And the view," she commented, "holding her arms out in front of her. Look at that blue water, and we can see straight across the bay to Petoskey on the other side."

"I think two glasses of wine at dinner was one too many for someone," Jason teased her as he put his arm around her waist and led her across the street to the city boat docks.

Kylie wrapped her arm comfortably behind his back, and he pulled her close as they slowly strolled past the sailboats and yachts. As they neared the end of the main city dock, they saw an older couple seated on a park bench at the end.

"Ah," Kylie sighed happily. "I hope I still have that much passion in me when I'm that age."

"Wow, they're really going at it," Jason observed.

"Yeah," she let out a happy sigh. "Love, sweet love."

"I think I recognize that guy's baseball cap," Jason started to say out loud to himself.

Just then the couple came up for air.

"Aunt Judy!" Kylie yelled louder than she meant to.

"Sam!" Jason echoed her shock.

The older couple turned sheepish faces to the younger

couple.

"Why, Kylie, what are you doing down here?" Judy asked, wiping the smeared lipstick from around her mouth. "I thought you said you were going out to dinner."

"We finished," Kylie answered, her mouth hanging open.

Sam was all smiles.

Stepping closer, Kylie whispered loudly, "What is wrong with you two?"

Judy's look of bliss left her face. "Well, I guess I have you to thank for that, Kylie Sue."

"What do you mean?"

"I saw the story about the Indian tea on your computer. I know what you intentionally fed me."

"Did you give her a Love Spell cupcake?" Jason asked accusingly.

"Love Spell?" Sam echoed.

"What?" Kylie looked at Jason. "No."

"She gave you one," Judy informed Sam.

"She did?"

"Yes. When you were at the nursing home in recovery."

"But I don't believe in spells," he began.

"And now she's given me some kind of acceptance cupcake," Judy smarted. "Didn't you wonder why I suddenly can't keep my hands off of you?"

"Acceptance cupcake?" Jason asked.

"Yes," Judy retorted. "The Native Americans used to use it when they were being courted. When a man would play his flute outside a woman's wigwam all night, it was like a marriage proposal. If she accepted, she would bring out this – this – " she struggled for the word " – tea." She looked at Jason. "It was a special tea."

"Like a love spell?" Jason asked.

"I don't believe in spells," Sam echoed again, holding up an index finger.

"It's an acceptance of love," Judy told Jason.

Judy turned back to Sam. "Did you notice how you just fell

in love with me after you ate the cupcake Kylie brought you a few months ago?"

Sam looked confused. "I just thought it was nice that you sent me a cupcake. I've always had my eye on you." He shrugged before continuing. "I just thought that the cupcake meant that you finally noticed me, too."

Kylie felt her heart melt for Sam.

"You always had your eye on me?" Judy asked.

"Since I saw you with the Girl Scouts in the parade."

Judy remembered volunteering when Kylie was with her in the summer. Her voice softened. "You remember that?"

Sam smiled sweetly. "Buttercup, I remember everything about you."

"So it wasn't a spell?" Judy asked, her anger melting.

"I didn't need a spell to notice you. I just thought you finally noticed me back."

Jason looked at Kylie accusingly but didn't say anything.

"Oh, Sam," Judy said, taking his face in her hands. "That's

the sweetest thing anyone has ever said to me." She leaned forward, giving him a long kiss, and Sam's arms wrapped back around her.

"Whew, I'm lucky that thing worked out," Kylie said, making her eyes large for emphasis as the younger couple turned from the public display of affection and started back down the dock.

"Kylie, you've got to stop slipping people things and meddling."

"Well, I didn't think it would actually work," she defended herself.

"Apparently, it does."

She slowed her step to look up to the firefighter. "Don't tell me that you believe in spells now, Chief Lange."

He looked adoringly down at her. "Well, I don't know if I believe in spells, but you sure do seem to meddle in people's love life."

She snaked her hand around his arm and hugged it. "I just like happy endings."

"Just for the record, you've never slipped me anything, right?"

She looked taken aback. "Chief Lange, I thought you said you didn't need a love spell when it came to me."

He smiled confidently. "I don't, but I was just checking."

She nudged his shoulder with her head as they walked by the endless parade of boats lining the long dock. "I haven't slipped you anything."

As they walked around a large group walking down the dock, she pulled away from him and stepped to the edge of the high dock.

"What are you doing?"

"Looking for fish," she replied as she leaned over the edge to gaze into the clear water below before a hand gripped her upper arm. "Ow," she turned back to him.

"Just be careful."

She hesitated, looked at his hand gripping her upper arm, and pointed her finger at it. "Uh, uh, uh, no rescuing."

"You would have to fall to be rescued."

"Well, no preventing rescuing," she corrected.

Undaunted by her favorite argument to start with him, he maintained his strong grip and pulled her away from the edge and to him. "I wouldn't want my girl to get messed up if she fell in."

Distracted from her rescuing rant, she hesitated before asking, "Your girl?"

"My girl," he repeated, still holding her close enough that their chests touched.

Her eyes held his as his free arm wrapped around her waist to secure her next to him. "Does that mean we're not seeing other people?"

He smiled his wide smile at her. "I didn't know we were ever seeing other people."

She felt color rush into her cheeks but didn't look away. "Oh." She felt her stomach begin to turn nervously as his lips came to hers, and he kissed her deeply. Forgetting they were in public, her hand moved up and around his neck as she returned his kiss, and she felt a wave of weakness rush through her.

When he finally pulled away, he told her, "I think I should stay at your place tonight."

The passion left her eyes and was replaced by surprise. "Huh? You mean sleep over?"

"It's been two months."

"You're counting?"

He grinned confidently. "Since Day One."

Her eyes jumped from side to side as she tried to think of an excuse. "But Cupcake will be there."

"She can watch," he kidded her with a grin as he kissed her again and she gave up on excuses and lost herself in the moment.

CHAPTER 28

Kylie awoke the next morning wearing Jason's crisp white dinner shirt. At first, she lay on her back, looking at the ceiling, trying to remember what had happened. When she heard a light snoring sound, she turned her head to see Fire Chief Jason Lange lying in bed next to her, his fabulously toned chest exposed. Her eyes followed the sound to the foot of the bed where Cupcake lay curled up and snoring in the REM stage of sleep.

Rolling onto her side to take in his strong physique without his knowledge, she reached out and lightly ran her fingertip over his large shoulder and down to the bicep.

His eyes didn't open, but he smiled. "Good morning." He continued to lay with his eyes closed.

"Good morning," she replied, rolling onto her stomach in the white shirt and propping herself up on her elbows to continue to watch him.

Her eyes took in his tanned torso with a light spattering of hair covering it. They followed it up to the arm that was wrapped behind his head. His light brown hair was disheveled, and her eyes moved down past his freckles to rest on his full lips as they spoke again.

"You're not staring at me as I sleep, are you?"

"No," she lied, smirking and turning her focus to her hands in front of her.

"So what are you thinking about?" he asked, his eyes still closed.

"The jingle dancer and the dog."

"And what about it?" He stretched to his full length, straightening his arms, but his eyes still remained closed.

Kylie looked down to Cupcake stirring at the foot of the bed as she spoke. "Dogs are loyal."

"Common knowledge."

"So what if the dog in the cave was her dog?"

He was silent for a moment. "The jingle dancer's dog?"

"Yeah."

"It's possible."

"What if someone shot her, and she crawled into that cave to hide from them?"

"It's possible."

Kylie looked back to Jason as she came to her final conclusion. "What if her dog wouldn't leave her side and died next to her?" Her voice had a sad tone to it as she finished.

"That's a lot of 'what ifs,'" Jason told her.

Kylie looked back to Cupcake. "Cupcake wants to be with me all the time. I think she'd stay with me if I was injured."

"Cupcake ditched you for a deer."

Kylie lightly swatted his arm but then immediately returned her hand to run it over his shoulder and to his prominent pectoral muscle. "I think she'd stay with me," she said thoughtfully as she lightly ran her fingers over his chest.

Jason rolled onto his side, snaked his arm around her waist, and pulled her to him before rolling back onto his back, pulling her on top of him. "I'd stay with you," he told her, nuzzling his nose against her cheek before kissing it.

"Well," she said playfully as each arm moved under one of his shoulders to pull him closer, "I was kind of counting on that."

CHAPTER 29

Onadesh threw open the deerskin flap to the wigwam and stepped inside unannounced. "Muckwa has returned?"

Immediately, Muckwa left the food being fed to him and started to bark at Onadesh, his front feet bouncing inches off the ground with each bark.

"Yes, I am here, boy, and we will find Little Fawn," Onadesh reassured the dog as he dropped to his knees to stroke its head.

Seconds of silence ticked by before Little Fawn's grandmother spoke. "Muckwa would not leave Little Fawn if she were alive. He is very devoted to her."

Onadesh shook his head. "No, she is alive. She must be alive." He turned his focus to the fluffy dog. "Muckwa, where is Wa-wash-ay-wesh Koons?"

Muckwa started his bouncy bark again.

"I must find her, Muckwa," he told the dog, who continued to bark.

"She is not with us anymore," the old woman told him. "I

feel it."

Onadesh shook his head again. "That is not so, is it, Muckwa?"

Muckwa barked again.

Onadesh rose from the dog. "We will find her, Muckwa. Come, take me to Wa-wash-ay-wesh Koons." He lifted the flap to the wigwam, and Muckwa darted out, pausing to bark at him in a high-pitched bark once they were outside the wigwam.

"Take me to her, Muckwa," Onadesh told the dog.

Muckwa ran towards the woods and then turned back, barking to Onadesh.

"I am coming, Muckwa," he told the dog as he chased it into the forest.

Muckwa ran ahead on the trail through the forest, always pausing and waiting for Onadesh to catch up.

"Good boy. That's it, take me to her," Onadesh reassured the dog as he followed tirelessly.

When Muckwa led him back to where the wall was being

built to hold in the Muscodesh bodies, Onadesh felt his heart sink.

Muckwa ran to the edge of the ravine near the pool and barked.

Onadesh slowed to a sad walk and approached the dog. Kneeling, he dropped his head to the animal's head. "Yes, Muckwa, she was here, but now she has disappeared."

Muckwa barked.

Onadesh rubbed his sweaty head against Muckwa's, seeking the only consolation he could think of. "She is not here, Muckwa. I have personally looked at every body that was placed behind that wall three times, and she is not among them." Emotion began to overwhelm him, and he wrapped his arms around the dog, despite the other Odawa men still working who might see him.

Muckwa wriggled free and ran to the edge of the pond, barking.

"Yes, Muckwa. That is where she was." His voice cracked as he thought of the rest of the sentence and whispered, "That is where she was when I struck her with an arrow."

Muckwa ran into the thick undergrowth and then back to

Onadesh, barking again.

"She is not here, Muckwa." He walked to the shallow pool and looked into it. "Not even her reflection is here," he said, dropping next to the large dog and placing his arm around it.

Muckwa let out a yip, ran again into the underbrush and back out. Stopping, he yipped again.

Exasperated, Onadesh stood and walked to where the dog waited and pushed aside a few of the small trees that lined the back of the pool. Turning back to the dog, he said, "See, she is not here, Muckwa. She was, but now she has disappeared."

Muckwa ran deeper into the underbrush and yipped again.

"You are at the wall to the ravine, Muckwa. Come, we will look for her elsewhere."

Muckwa stood in the bushes and yipped again.

Onadesh shook his head sadly. "You, my friend, must have been as traumatized as I when you saw what I did to her." He shook his head sadly. "You are losing your mind."

Muckwa yipped again from amongst the bushes.

Onadesh lowered his body again next to the small pool and dropped his head into his hands. "I will not rest until I find her, Muckwa. Whether she is alive or dead, I will walk the Earth until I find her."

Muckwa let out another yip, and Onadesh dropped his head lower, his fingertips running over his shaved skull and squeezing his head as he began to rock his body in sorrow.

CHAPTER 30

"What's a Wasson Hill?" Kylie called from the kitchen, standing at the stove and flipping pancakes in the large, white dress shirt Jason had worn to dinner the night before.

"No idea."

She flipped a pancake and placed the spatula on top of it. "Hey, you're the lifetime local person. You're supposed to know this stuff."

A few seconds ticked by, and she flipped another pancake.

"It might be a person's name," he said from the doorway to the kitchen.

Kylie turned to see him standing in his boxers, hair rumpled.

She threw him a half grin as she took in the view.

He left the door frame, crossed the room in a couple of steps, and wrapped his arms around her. First kissing her ear, his whispered into it, "You look amazing."

"I'm a mess," she whispered, turning her head to give him a quick kiss before returning her focus to the pancakes.

He squeezed her harder. "Amazing."

She flipped another pancake on the large stovetop grill.

"These aren't Love Spell pancakes, are they?" he asked cautiously.

She turned her head sideways so her eyes could meet his. "I thought you didn't need them?"

"I don't. I just like to know what I'm eating."

She slipped the spatula under a pancake and put it onto a plate.

"These are nothing special. Just your basic peaches and cream pancakes."

"Peaches and cream?" he queried into her ear.

"Peaches and ricotta cheese."

"Mmm."

She flipped another pancake. "So you don't know these Wasson people?"

"Nope. Where is this coming from?"

"From the poem Sam pointed out to me in the library."

"Ah, we're back to this," he acknowledged, loosening his embrace around her waist.

"Well, I just want to know what the deal is," she told him, placing the rest of the pancakes onto the stack.

"Do you have syrup?" he asked, glancing around.

"There's a mild balsamic syrup in that little, white pitcher over there," she said absentmindedly.

"Balsamic?" he wrinkled up his nose and made a face.

She let out an impatient sigh. "Just trust me, you'll like it." She reached to the counter, lifted a small, white dish, and set it next to his plate.

They each sat on a stool at the end of the long, stainless steel island in her chef's kitchen.

"Mmm, what's this?" he asked through a mouthful of dry pancake as he tilted the white bowl and inspected it.

"It's whipped butter."

He raised his eyebrows to her. "Wow, you really go all out."

She smiled at him and poked a pancake from the stack with

her fork, dropping it onto her own plate. "So, back to the poem," she prefaced, "it says something winds across the old mill-creek."

He shrugged, pocketed the pancake into his cheek, and said, "A stream."

"Right," she said, holding up her fork. "That's what I thought at first, too; but since when does a stream cross a creek?"

He shrugged. "Maybe a road?"

"And why would the words 'mill' and 'creek' be hyphenated?"

"Typo?" he asked as he swallowed the large mouthful and cut another chunk from the stack on his plate with the side of his fork.

Kylie reached for the poem on the island and slid it closer. "Mmm, I doubt it."

"This is really good," he said, cramming more pancake into his mouth.

"I told you to trust me," she replied without looking up from the poem in front of her. "It could be the ravine that winds across the mill-creek," she tapped her fingertips on the table as she thought, "or a path or road, as you said." She ignored her pancakes. "But that still doesn't explain why 'mill-creek' is hyphenated."

"Have you made this flavor cupcake?"

"Huh?" She looked up from the poem.

"Have you sold this flavor cupcake in your shop yet?"

She smiled, happy he appreciated what she had made. "No, I don't think so."

Still speaking with his mouth full, he said, "You totally should."

"And what would I call it?" She acted as if she was deep in thought. "Peaches and cream sounds so simplistic." She looked at the ceiling and tapped her fingertips thoughtfully on her chin.

"Well, since it was my idea to make it into a cupcake," he said, reaching his fork to the stack and successfully stabbing another pancake, "I think you should call it The Jason."

Kylie grinned at him. "I don't think anyone would know

what flavor that was."

He spread the whipped butter on the pancake before pouring some syrup on it. "Good point." He threw her a sideways glance and pointed the fork at her. "So I suppose The Chief and The Firefighter would be eliminated as possible names also?"

Her dimples deepened. "I think so."

"I'm telling you," he said, cutting another large bite, "I could get used to this."

She smiled and placed her hand affectionately on his bare thigh as he continued to eat, turning her focus back to the poem. "So the next line says, 'A wall is laid to old walls, to hold the Hurdle Bend.'"

Jason shook his head, his mouth still full. "There's no wall there. We would have seen it."

Kylie tapped the prongs of her fork lightly against her bottom lip. "Unless it was buried."

"By what?"

She shrugged. "Washout." Her eyes moved to the top of

the page. "This poem was written in the 1920s. That's almost a hundred years ago. A lot could have happened between then and now."

Using the tip of his fork, he moved the last bite of pancake around on his plate, soaking up the last drop of syrup. "So let's say, in the 1920s, a reinforcing wall was built," he paused to gesture "so what" with his hands before finishing, "what's the big deal?"

"I'm not sure," Kylie mused, studying the words.

"Are you going to eat that?"

She looked up to see him pointing to her plate with his fork, and she held up her hand dismissively. "No, go ahead." She looked back at the poem. "So, if that's what it means, then who built the first wall, and why?"

He stabbed the pancake and put it on his own plate. Spreading the last of the whipped butter, he answered, "Just what the poem says. After heavy rain, it got washed out."

"Hmm, maybe," she said slowly before turning to look at him. "So will you go out there with me today to have a look around?"

He pocketed a piece of pancake in his cheek again. "Oh, so now you want me to go along?"

"Well, I might need someone to dig."

His eyebrows arched. "Dig?"

"Give me a piece of that," she said reaching over and tearing off some of the pancake he'd taken from her plate.

"Hey," his voice cracked. "You suddenly want some, and it's the last one?"

"No," she smiled calmly at him, "Cupcake wants some." She leaned over and handed the piece to the puppy sitting patiently next to her feet.

"Hey," his voice cracked again. "That's too good for the dog!"

Kylie smiled and looked at the puppy who happily sat thumping her tail. "Hmm, what do you think of that Cuppie? The mean ol' fire chief doesn't want to share with you."

Cupcake let out a yip, and Kylie turned back to Jason.

"Bad news."

"What?"

"She wants more."

Jason looked alarmed as he wrapped his strong arms protectively around the plate. "No." He looked around, worried. "Don't you have bacon or something for her?"

Kylie grinned happily and leaned in to kiss his cheek. "Did I tell you good morning yet?"

Distracted more easily than she had expected, he swallowed the remaining pancake in his mouth, leaned forward, and gave her a long, slow kiss. Pulling back and forgetting about the pancakes, he said, "It's afternoon."

CHAPTER 31

Onadesh and Nakoma stood poised at the top of the bluff, lined up along the edge with the rest of the group. Behind him he heard the drums beating as the Midewiwin chanted. Below them, the stench of quickly-rotting corpses wafted up. Others stood next to the wall of logs built high to hold in the bodies and all of their Muscodesh belongings. Looking down at his fellow Odawa, Onadesh could see the masks they wore in an attempt to filter out the stench so close to them.

"All at once!" Onadesh yelled to the men on the cliff.

Lifting the sticks with the wide, flat-headed points at the end, they hesitated.

Onadesh took a final look below before yelling, "Now!"

At once, the men lining the edge of the bluff began to chop the ground, digging the flat-headed instruments into it until large chunks of soil broke free.

"Keep going!" he called to them.

The onlookers below stepped back as yards upon yards of

soil broke free from the cliff and fell onto the corpses.

When the upper level was cleared, Onadesh instructed them to step down to the next solid level, and the process was repeated as a hundred tools cut into the soil like a small earthquake that quickly eroded another section of the bluff. When they were finished, what had once been a small ravine became a very narrow and deep ravine at the top. The bottom, however, sloped more gently than it had previously.

After many hours, covered in sweat, Onadesh was satisfied that the Muscodesh and the smell that drifted into the surrounding area from their bodies were gone.

Wiping his brow with the back of his hand, he stopped his work and nodded. "The task is complete. The Muscodesh are no more."

Nakoma slapped his friend on the back. "Let's go have a swim before we go back to the village."

Onadesh, his eyes hard again, shook his head. "You go. You have worked hard. I will stay and," he thought for his excuse, "make sure things are properly finished."

Nakoma looked around them at the people readily leaving the site before returning his gaze to his friend. "It is good, Onadesh." His voice softened. "You cannot stay here and look for Little Fawn forever. She is gone."

"She did not disappear into thin air," he said through his teeth, holding back his anger that was thinly veiled due to his sheer exhaustion.

"Well, she is not here."

"Go." Onadesh gave his friend a hard push towards the village. "Go."

Nakoma stumbled and looked back. "If she did not disappear, then she is not here, Onadesh. Look elsewhere."

Onadesh turned his back and started to walk into the dense forest of the ravine and away from the mass grave.

"Maybe the Muscodesh took her," Nakoma suggested, calling after his friend. "Maybe she is in the lake."

Onadesh did not turn. "I know what I saw," he whispered to

himself as he walked calmly into the forest.

"Maybe she went back to Manitoulin Island," Nakoma called weakly to his friend as the distance grew between them. "Go look for her there." Onadesh kept walking. His friend was nearly out of Nakoma's sight when Nakoma said softly, "She could be anywhere."

Onadesh disappeared into the forest.

Alone at the grave site, Nakoma looked up into the treetops around him that let the waning light through. He listened. Not a bird or any sound could be heard. Looking to where his friend had disappeared one last time, Nakoma turned and ran back to the village.

Onadesh followed the small creek up the ravine to its head and the spot where he had first laid eyes on Little Fawn. He had eaten little since he'd gone to war with the Muscodesh, but his body no longer felt hunger.

With a loud scream from his broken heart, he exerted a super-human effort and rolled a large boulder into the creek. Satisfied, he stepped back and repeated the process with another boulder. He did it again and again until a small pool formed and the creek no longer ran through the ravine and onto the grave. The water would be safe.

Fashioning a crude shelter, he laid down and slept for the first time in days. He slept long and hard. When he awoke, he began his search anew, scouring the forest and the bluff looking for Little Fawn. Day after day and night after night he searched alone. Eventually, this became all that was left of the chief's son and a once-great warrior. True to his name, his people saw him wandering, and it was most often in the moonlight. No one knew when Onadesh died, and some say he never did.

CHAPTER 32

Kylie held Jason's hand as they waited in the long line that curved through the popular sandwich shop in town.

"It's 1:30," she pointed out. "Don't these people have to be back at work?"

"There's a line here from the time they open until the time they close," Jason told her.

"How do I get all of these people to cross the street to the cupcake shop for dessert?" Kylie wondered aloud, and Jason smiled. "You know, we could just go get a couple of cupcakes from the shop for lunch instead of waiting in line."

Jason put his hand on her low back and eased her forward in the line. "Believe me, it's worth the wait. And, since you may have me digging a new tunnel back to your house, I thought we should get some sustenance." She crossed her arms impatiently. "Plus," he added, "I could use some protein to offset all of that sugar for breakfast."

She smiled and poked him in the ribs with the elbow of one

of her crossed arms.

The front screen door to the shop loudly creaked open, and a familiar face stepped in.

Jason raised his hand in greeting, and Aaron crossed over to them.

"Wow, it's a long line today," he commented, casually slipping his hands into the front pockets of his shorts.

"We're almost to the front. Give me your order, and I'll place it with ours," Jason offered.

"Thanks." Aaron looked the couple up and down. "It's a little warm for jeans, don't you think?"

"We're headed back out to Devil's Elbow to poke around," Jason said casually.

Aaron raised his eyebrows to Kylie. "I'm surprised you want to go back after making the news the other night."

Kylie blushed. "I still have the walking cast on until tomorrow, but it's doing a lot better."

"Looking for more bodies or just ghosts this time?"

"The ghosts happen during the hours of darkness," Kylie reminded him, holding up a finger. "We plan to be in and out in a couple of hours."

"So what are you looking for this time?" Aaron asked, stepping into the line beside them and ignoring the looks of disapproval from the people behind him.

"A wall," Jason said in a patronizing tone.

"A wall?" Aaron looked from Jason to Kylie.

Kylie narrowed her eyes, trying to discern how much he really knew. "Have you heard about a wall out there?"

Looking completely uninformed, Aaron shook his head. "Why do you think there is one?"

Kylie pulled a crumpled piece of paper from her pocket, unfolded it, and handed it to Aaron. "Just an old poem I found in the library."

Aaron began mumbling from the top of the page to himself.

"Here," Kylie said, leaning in to him and pointing, "skip to this part."

Aaron read the stanzas to himself as they took another step forward in the long line. "So what's it mean?" he asked, looking up.

Kylie's face fell. "I was hoping you could tell us."

He shrugged. "It's all rhyming gibberish to me."

Kylie took the poem back from him and looked at it. "Okay. For example, what's a Wasson?"

"That part I do know," Aaron said.

"And…?" she prompted.

"It's the name of a local Native American family that used to own that stretch of land around Seven Mile Point."

"Seven Mile Point?" Kylie asked, her mind searching for a memory of the location.

"It's south of Devil's Elbow," Jason told her.

"How far south?"

"A few miles." Jason looked to Aaron for agreement.

"It's just south of where The Tunnel of Trees begins," Aaron told her.

"Ah," Kylie responded, disappointed. "So that's not really in our area." She looked back down at the paper. "And the mill-creek? Do you know where that is?"

Aaron tilted his head to the ceiling in thought for a moment. "There used to be an old mill on M-119. It was on Five Mile Creek. Maybe that's the one the poet is talking about."

"That would be closer to Seven Mile Point," Jason agreed.

Kylie's heart sunk further. "But still not in our area." She looked back down at the poem. "A wall is laid to old walls." She looked back up to Aaron. "Do you know of a wall anywhere out there? Maybe one built in the 1920s?"

Aaron followed Jason as he stepped forward in the line. "Nothing I can think of but, again, it sounds like he's talking about the area south of Devil's Elbow."

Kylie looked down at the paper. "But it says it's holding the Hurdle Bend, and those words are capitalized like it's the name of a place. Are there any big bends in the road along Seven Mile Point like in The Tunnel of Trees?"

Aaron looked to Jason for confirmation, and Jason shook his

head. Turning back to Kylie, he said, "No. That road is low and runs along the water, so it's fairly straight."

"At least there are no death-defying turns in the road like Horseshoe Bend or Devil's Elbow," Jason agreed, referring to the two sharpest turns in The Tunnel of Trees. "Tell him what you want," Jason told Kylie as they finally reached the counter.

Kylie placed her fingertips over the chest-high counter of the sandwich shop. "I'll have a turkey on white with Swiss cheese and extra mayo." The person behind the counter worked silently before placing a Saran-wrapped sandwich on the countertop.

"Go ahead," Jason told Aaron.

"I'll have a Trainwreck on whole wheat with mustard," Aaron said, referring to the most popular sandwich sold in the shop that was a combination of different meats.

Seconds later, another Saran-wrapped sandwich appeared on the counter, and the sandwich-maker looked to Jason. "What can I get you?"

"The same thing only with mayo," Jason told him.

Each grabbing their sandwich, they moved to the shorter line formed at the cash register.

"So are you still going?" Aaron asked.

"Heck, yeah," Kylie said. "I've got to do it while I have a digger." She pointed a thumb to Jason.

"I'm sure it's private property, so you should ask permission from whoever lives around there."

"Oh." Kylie felt her heart sink again. "I didn't think of that."

"Doesn't the Road Commission own the area a certain distance from the road?" Jason asked Aaron.

Aaron shrugged. "I'm not sure, but you should probably check into it before you go digging up someone's backyard."

"A very good point," Jason said, throwing Kylie a look.

"Do you want a pickle?" the owner's son asked them as he punched the sums into the cash register.

"Yes," came the reply from all three.

"I think I'll go grab a cupcake from Judy to wash this down," Aaron told them as they walked out the back door to the parking lot.

"Just don't get the Mint Energy Zinger or whatever it's called," Jason warned him.

"Energy?" he asked, raising his eyebrows. "Is that like one of those drinks with mega amounts of caffeine only in a cupcake?"

"Not exactly," Jason commented dryly as he received an elbow nudge from Kylie.

"If it's meant to be..." Kylie said with a wise expression on her face as Jason pulled open the passenger door to his truck.

"Hey!" Aaron called.

Kylie turned away from the truck to see him jogging back across the parking lot towards them.

"This probably doesn't mean anything to you but, ever since I was a kid, we were told to stay away from Devil's Elbow."

"Why?" Kylie asked, her eyes widening.

He shook his head. "We never thought to ask. It was just one of those things that you did as you were told."

Kylie felt a shiver ripple up her spine upon hearing the

ominous warning.

"Anyway, I don't really know the reason for it, but just be careful. Take your cell phones with you in case you need help."

Kylie looked up at Jason. "There's no cell reception in the ravine."

CHAPTER 33

"I think not bringing Cupcake along today was one of your better moves," Jason told Kylie as they got out of his truck at the base of the ravine.

Kylie glanced at the opening in front of them. "This place creeps her out." She looked to Jason as he put on his headlamp and pulled the shovel out of the back of his truck. "Aunt Judy needed some company at the shop besides Sam today."

"I think Sam is going to be your next employee."

"He does spend a lot of time at the shop," Kylie acknowledged as she started up the deer path into the ravine.

"I'm sure he'd give you a great deal," Jason teased. "Maybe something like working in exchange for time with Judy."

Kylie thought a moment as they walked up the path, surrounded by the leaves that were beginning to exchange their summer green for colors of fire. "You don't believe they're together because of some food combination that I found on the internet, do you?"

"Maybe that's what broke the ice, but it seems Sam's always had a genuine interest in your aunt."

"Yeah," she agreed. "So it can't go wrong, right? It'll be okay?"

Jason started to understand where she was going. "You're afraid Judy will get hurt, aren't you?"

Kylie shrugged as she pushed a small branch out of the way and held it until Jason passed. "I just don't want her to be alone."

Jason reached behind himself and grasped her hand in his. As you just said, "Whatever will be, will be. You can't control it."

"No, but maybe I can help it along a little." His large hand gave hers a squeeze. "I just want it to last," she concluded.

"I think that's up to them," Jason commented.

Kylie's mind was spinning. "Maybe so."

The couple followed the winding path to the small pool at the base of the cliff that matched the one at the top of the ravine.

"So where are you thinking a wall would be, madam?"

Kylie put a hand on her hip while she used the other one to

pinch her lower lip with two fingers as her eyes slowly surveyed the area. "See how the cliff is so steep here and here?" she pointed to the sides.

"Yeah."

She pointed to the center that sloped down from the road above more gently. "Versus over here, where it's more gradual.

"Yep. Probably not where you're going to need a retaining wall." He turned to the steep sides and stepped up to one. "So you want me to start digging over on this steep part?"

Kylie's eyes were still darting from side to side. "Yeah, I guess," she said hesitantly.

Jason stepped to the side opposite the small cave where the body had been found and began to poke his shovel into the cliff, hoping to hit something solid, as Kylie stepped back to get a better look at the area.

"The weird thing is," she pointed out as he dug, "that the entire bluff, as far as I can see, is very steep, except for this part." She pointed to the center again.

Jason paused his poking. "There really isn't much need for a wall over there."

Kylie continued to pinch her lip as she looked back and forth at the different inclines. "Yeah. It's just weird." She turned back to Jason. "Keep checking where you are, and let's see what we find."

"Your wish is my command, my lady," he teased as he scooped a heavy shovelful of soil from the cliff.

Kylie stood behind him and peered into the small hole. "I just see more dirt."

"Kind of what I expected to find."

She pinched her lower lip again as her eyes scanned the area. "Hold on." She walked gingerly in her walking cast to the center of the ravine with its gradual incline. "'It has a wash to fill,'" she recited, looking up the slope. "Maybe it's not as steep here because it's been washed out."

"Maybe."

Kylie walked to the base and started pushing baby trees aside. Following her lead, Jason moved to the other corner and did the same.

"Ah-ha!" Kylie called after taking a few steps up the incline. "A wall!" She pointed to a thick stone wall whose top emerged from the dirt.

Jason looked up the ravine and followed the angle down. "The washout must have eventually overcome the wall and buried it."

"'A wall is laid to old walls,'" Kylie recited the poem. She pointed just up the incline from the top of the stone wall. "So there must be another wall in this area."

"Okay, so maybe there's another wall. So what?" Jason asked.

"Because I want to know who built it."

"Probably the same people that built the road."

Kylie put her hands on her hips. "And who do you think would have built a road out here that needed to be repaired by the 1920s?"

"Native Americans."

"Right."

"So I just saved myself a lot of digging. We know who built it."

"But why?"

"Uh," he hesitated, "the same reason the new wall was built. To prevent washout."

Kylie squished her cheeks up to her eyes. "Why would Native Americans care if the ravine washed out? Why this ravine in this spot? I'm sure there were lots of spots that washed out along this bluff."

Jason's eyes drifted to where the small cave lay hidden. "So you think it may have something to do with our jingle dancer?"

"Are all cupcakes better with frosting?"

He smiled and shook his head. "Okay, I see where you're going. Let me run back to the truck and get something."

"I'll go with you," she said, sinking her walking cast into the incline she had ascended.

"No, Gimpy, you hang tight." He lifted his shovel and sunk it into the ground. "I'll be right back."

"No, Jason!" she called after him. "Don't leave me alone here."

"You'll be fine," he called over his shoulder. "I'll be faster without you limping along. It will just be a minute."

Kylie looked around the silent ravine and shivered. "What if that man comes back?" she asked in a soft voice that she knew Jason couldn't hear as he jogged down the trail. She sat down on the incline, most of her body disappearing into the small trees lining the hillside. "This is why I should have brought Cupcake with me," she mumbled.

A gentle breeze rustled the maple saplings that grew close to the edges, and Kylie's attention was drawn to the pond that sat in front of where the body was found.

Kylie lifted an arm and rolled her fingertips against her chin. "I wonder if there's anything left in there that the coroner's office missed." Her eyes darted to the trail and saw no sign of Jason. Standing, she took a couple of steps down the hill when she heard a drum beat. Turning her head to look up the bluff, she heard a car driving by.

"It's just the echo from the car on the road," she whispered to herself as she felt beads of sweat pop out on her chest. Her eyes looked around, now filled with fear, and she dropped back onto her bottom, allowing the underbrush to hide her. Her hands dropped to her sides. Feeling the ground beneath her, her fingertips dug into it and scooped it into her palms.

She heard a whisper behind her before there was a loud snapping sound. "The voices," she whispered to herself, as a wave of terror swept through her body.

Her heart stopped in her chest, Kylie turned towards the sound.

"I'm tempted to just shoot."

Frozen in her seated position, Kylie saw a woman standing in a long, white nightgown, her long, gray hair blowing lightly in the breeze. One eye was closed, and the other peered at Kylie through the rear sight and down the barrel of a rifle.

"I've cocked the rifle, and I'll shoot if you don't move on out of here."

Kylie was unable to speak as she slowly lifted her hands, dropping the dirt as she did so.

The woman watched her closely through the rear sight of the gun. "You're one of them gold hunters, aren't ya?"

Slowly rising to a stand, Kylie opened her mouth but could only shake her head.

"Either that or ya heard about the Indian burial ground."

Kylie's ability to speak returning, she asked, "Burial ground?"

"Don't play dumb with me, Missy. I've got two rounds in this here gun, and I'm not afraid to use them."

Kylie tilted her head and looked at the woman. "Do I know you?"

The woman with the gun took a step closer. "I'll tell you the same thing I've told the others that have been here looking for Lord knows what. I'll give you to the count of ten, and then I'll aim at your feet and shoot."

"Mrs. Swift?" Jason interrupted.

The woman's focus left Kylie as she swung the gun to Jason. "Lucky you're here, Chief. I've caught this young lady trespassing on my land." She swung the gun back towards Kylie. "I'm about to do a good ol' boy's form of a citizen's arrest."

"You're right, Mrs. Swift. We were – " Jason began.

Kylie held up her hand to interrupt him. "Remember our talk?"

Jason pinched his lips together and held out a hand, indicating for her to go ahead.

Looking at the woman, she asked, "Mrs. Swift? Stella Swift?"

Not lowering the gun, she answered, "Yeah. What about it?"

Kylie relaxed a little and placed her hand on her chest. "I'm Kylie Branson, Judy's niece."

"Judy?" Stella didn't lower the weapon.

"Yes. I was in your Girl Scout troop when I spent summers

here."

"Hmm, yes, Kylie." Stella nodded but didn't lower the weapon.

Relieved she was recognized, Kylie continued. "Yes. Remember, you helped us earn our badge on marksmanship?"

"Ah, yes," the old woman responded. "You were a good shot." She gave a tiny shrug. "I guess it won't all be wasted if I have to blow your foot off for not getting off of my land."

"What?"

"You heard me."

Kylie gave a slight eye roll. "Oh, come on, Mrs. Swift. People don't really do that. This isn't the wild west."

"Kylie, I think you should – " Jason began.

Kylie snapped her head at him. "Hey, I said I've got – " She was interrupted by a bullet shooting into the ground next to her walking cast.

"Hey!" she squealed, taking a small jump to the side. "Troop leaders don't shoot Girl Scouts!"

"Get off that sacred land before my aim improves."

Kylie looked at Jason with frightened eyes. Crossing his arms, he smirked and shook his head, letting her handle the situation as she had requested.

"Okay, okay." Keeping her focus on Mrs. Swift and her hands up, Kylie side-stepped down the incline towards Jason.

Mrs. Swift followed her with the gun. "Now continue that step until you get to the road."

"But can't we ask you about it?" Kylie argued.

"I don't think this is the time to be making suggestions," Jason leaned in and whispered to her, his hands moving comfortably into his pockets.

"There's nothing to discuss. This here land doesn't belong to you." She hesitated. "Hell, it doesn't even belong to me."

Kylie looked at her with questions in her eyes. "Huh?"

"It belongs to the people who were here before us."

Jason took a step back and gave the back of Kylie's black, short-sleeved top a tug.

"You mean the jingle dancer we found?"

The woman's eyes narrowed suspiciously. "You're the one that found her?"

Kylie nodded, and Jason took another step back.

"So you were trespassing before, eh?"

Kylie held up an index finger. "Technically, that was my dog. We were just chasing her."

"So now everyone knows. I won't be able to keep anyone off of my land and let these poor people rest in peace."

"People?" Kylie picked up on the word.

Shaking her head, Stella dropped the rifle to her waist and gestured to the incline. "The Native Americans that rest here." She looked at the gradual incline and followed up more quietly, "And the ones that don't rest."

Kylie lowered her hands. "So it is haunted?"

Stella looked sad. "How can it not be with as many bodies as there are here?"

Kylie's eyes moved to the soil that nearly covered the stone wall. "Are they behind the stone wall that we found the top of?"

"I suppose." Her eyes sadly followed the slope from the top to the bottom. "Those that haven't washed away in heavy rains anyway."

Forgetting her fear, Kylie stepped forward as Jason lunged to tug on her shirt again in an effort to hold her back. "So you know for a fact that bodies were buried behind that wall?" she asked.

Stella nodded sadly. "Bodies and weapons and pottery and every sort of thing you can imagine."

Kylie took another step forward. "Have you dug it up?"

Stella snapped to her senses and looked at Kylie. "God, no. I wouldn't dig up anyone's resting place."

Kylie pushed her eyebrows together. "The local historian said there wasn't a burial ground here, nor were there any archeological findings."

"That they know of," Stella retorted. "If you don't tell anyone where to look, people won't know."

Kylie took a third step forward. "So you think it's some sort of ancient Indian burial ground?"

Stella lifted her shoulders and lowered them. "Something like that."

"Cool," Kylie mumbled, her eyes looking at the ground with new interest.

"And you were about to go and dig it all up," Stella said scornfully, turning her head to look at Kylie and Jason.

"Technically," Jason responded, "we weren't going to dig. We were going to use this." He leaned and retrieved a long gadget he had leaned against a tree.

Stella narrowed her eyes again. "A metal detector?"

"Yep," he responded proudly.

"A metal detector?" Kylie asked incredulously. "This is an ancient burial ground. There won't be metal here."

Jason lifted a finger to respond before he was cut off by Mrs. Swift.

"These weren't cavemen, Kylie," Stella informed her. "There were plenty of copper arrowheads and tools that washed out over the years in the heavy rain.

"Really?" Kylie asked.

"Sure," Stella informed. "We aren't that far from the Keweenaw Peninsula, and copper is abundant there. The Native Americans up there actually mined it using a melting technique."

"Oh, yeah?" Kylie asked with interest, taking another step forward. Snapping her fingers and pointing to Jason, "Our jingle dancer was killed by a copper arrowhead."

"I guess you didn't grasp that part of the Girl Scout program," Stella mumbled to herself.

Kylie threw her a sideways glance but didn't comment.

"The part I don't understand is, if this is a Native American burial ground, then why doesn't the local historian know about it?" Jason asked.

Stella looked to Jason. "The Native Americans used a verbal form of history-keeping. Everything was handed down in a story format. If the story wasn't handed down, he wouldn't know about it."

Kylie's mind was spinning as she pinched her lower lip between two fingers. "I think I know why he doesn't know about it."

CHAPTER 34

Kylie, Jason, Aaron, Judy, and Sam walked up the sidewalk made of paved field stones.

"I haven't seen Stella in years," Judy commented. "I'd forgotten that she lived this far out of town."

"And it's conveniently close to the ceremony," Sam said, holding Judy's hand.

Jason moved to the front of the group and rang the doorbell. Minutes ticked by, and no one responded.

"Are you sure she said she'd be here today?" Kylie asked Judy.

"Yes. She's going to the ceremony with us afterwards."

Seconds ticked by before the door was quickly opened. The group stood quietly taking in the woman before them in her riding habit, the once-wild hair swept into a chignon at the back of her head.

"Hi, Mrs. Swift," Jason started.

Stella eyed the group carefully before pointing her finger at them. "Everyone agrees, no one is to know about this?"

The group nodded silently, and Stella watched them carefully for a moment. Her eyes darted from side to side as if to check for others watching before motioning them into her large, white-sided house.

"Stella," Judy greeted her once fellow troop leader.

"Jude," Stella said with some familiarity. "Still hogging all of the cheese?"

Judy let a sound of dismissal escape her lips before gently swatting Stella's arm in jest.

"Come on, this way, kids," Stella said, motioning for the group to follow her.

Kylie followed the group through the large house, walking on Oriental rugs but noticing the intricately woven Native American blankets and artwork hanging on the walls. "Are these things you found on your property?" Kylie asked innocently.

"No," Stella threw over her shoulder.

Reaching a door on the south side of the house, Stella pulled a key from her pocket and unlocked it. Turning to the group in explanation, she said, "I believe these relics are pre European arrival," she watched them carefully as she spoke, "which makes them priceless."

When no one responded, she swung open the door to a sun room with shelf-lined walls from the waist down. Blinds of a papery-material hung over the windows to protect the archaeological findings from harsh rays.

Stella stepped into the room and held an arm out with a sweeping motion. "These are the relics my family has found over the years. We have collected them here," she turned, and her eyes looked sharply at Aaron, "and here they shall stay."

The group dispersed throughout the room to bend and look at the items on the low shelves.

"No touching!" Stella called after them.

"Here's a copper arrowhead," Kylie pointed.

"And beadwork," Judy said in awe.

Minutes passed as the group looked at the utensils, pottery, and other findings in the room; but it was Aaron who quietly focused on the pottery alone.

"May I?" he asked Stella before picking up a piece.

"What part of 'no touching' do you not understand?" Stella asked.

"I'll be very careful," Aaron assured her.

"Here, put this pillow under it when you hold it," Kylie said, grabbing a pillow off of one of the armchairs and putting it in front of Aaron in his kneeling position.

Stella shrugged and let out a sigh. "You break it, you buy it."

Aaron gently lifted the piece of pottery and looked on the bottom and then inside of it before setting it back on the shelf. Without saying a word to the others, he quietly looked at the rest of the pieces.

"So is it a clue?" Kylie asked.

Aaron rolled his lips tightly together and nodded.

"So can you read the inscriptions or understand the designs?" Kylie asked again.

Aaron shook his head.

"Well, why not?" Judy asked. "Aren't you the local tribal historian?"

Sam watched Aaron carefully before answering Judy for him. "My guess is the work isn't that of the Odawa nation."

"Well, who else's work would it be?" Judy asked, turning to Sam, who only threw a slight nod to turn attention to Aaron.

"You're right, this is not Odawa pottery," Aaron told the group.

"Well, who else would create this?" Stella asked, surprised. "I've studied a lot of the local history, and the Odawa are the only ones that lived on this side of the state."

Aaron held his lips tightly together for a moment again before he answered. "Legend has it that there was another tribe that the Odawa once shared their land with."

Kylie let out a gasp before saying, "The missing tribe."

Aaron nodded at her.

"There's a missing tribe?" Judy asked, looking to Stella for confirmation of the statement.

Stella only shook her head in confusion before looking to Aaron. "What was the name of the other tribe?"

Aaron looked sadly at the group before whispering, "The Muscodesh."

CHAPTER 35

The medicine man spoke quickly, and a man behind him accented certain words with a drum beat. The group stood back a short distance from the grave of the jingle dress dancer as the Midewiwin each took turns speaking. Kylie could hear the waves lapping against the Good Hart Beach as they stood in the nearby cemetery next to the Middle Village church.

"What are they saying?" Kylie leaned forward and whispered to Aaron.

"It is believed that the spirit lingers with the body until the Midewiwin give it guidance."

"So what kind of guidance?" Kylie asked.

Aaron listened for a moment before whispering back. "They are telling her to avoid certain turns in the road to the spirit land or which spirits to trust or not trust."

Kylie nodded and continued to watch until the drummer struck an especially loud beat, the last Mide spoke, there was one more beat of the drum, and then silence.

"What just happened?" Kylie whispered again, feeling Jason's soothing hand rubbing her back.

"He said, 'Your feet are now on the road of souls.'"

"So she's gone now?" Kylie asked again.

The Midewiwin and other tribal members stepped back, and the simple box containing the few remains of the jingle dress dancer was lowered into the ground.

"She can leave now. She has been put to rest," he whispered back.

Kylie looked around at the small cemetery of white crosses bearing no name marker. Her hand reached behind her back, grasped Jason's, and pulled it to her side.

Quietly, shovelfuls of dirt were dropped onto the remains; and the group watched sadly.

"So does that mean people will stop hearing the voices after dark out here?" Judy asked.

"I thought you didn't believe in that kind of thing," Kylie chided.

"I don't, but plenty of people talk about it."

Aaron turned away from the grave to face the group. "The Midewiwin will perform the same ceremony at the mass grave."

"So that will stop the voices after dark?" Judy asked again.

"And the drum beats," Sam added, lifting a finger.

Aaron nodded. "The souls will be able to leave if they wish."

Kylie shivered as she remembered the man she had seen in the woods. "Even the man with the hateful eyes that I saw at the head of the spring?"

Aaron met her eyes. "That is entirely up to him." He shrugged casually. "Maybe his purpose has been fulfilled."

"How could that be?" Kylie asked.

"Maybe he was guarding the graves. Maybe he was waiting for them to be found and laid to rest."

"Or maybe he was guarding the jingle dress dancer," Jason offered.

"Maybe he's just a super creepy ghost," Kylie muttered.

Aaron threw her a half smile. "He may choose to stay.

There is only one way to find out."

Kylie's eyes widened when she realized what he meant. "Don't look at me. I'm not going back up there."

"I'm sure the property owner will appreciate that," Jason commented dryly, and Kylie gently poked her elbow into his rib cage.

The group turned and slowly walked out of the cemetery and towards the parking lot.

Kylie, holding Jason's hand, pointed in front of them. "Looks like things might work out for Aunt Judy and Sam."

He gave her hand a gentle squeeze. "Judy holding anyone's hand is a good sign." He watched them as he took a few more steps. "It's still early, but they just might last."

"So maybe my Native American love-acceptance cupcakes were a good idea," she gloated.

"It depends on how many people in town ate them. You might have a lot of people in town chasing after each other if they ate your cupcakes."

She squeezed his hand back and threw him a dimpled smile. "Why, Chief Lange, are you saying that you believe in spells?" She held her hand out in front of her as if reading a billboard. "I can see the headlines now. 'Cupcake-maker casts love spell on small town. Hundreds –' no, wait, 'thousands fall in love.'"

He threw her one of his wide grins, stopped his walk, and pulled her to him. "So, now that you've cast your spell on me, what do you think about moving in together?"

Kylie snaked her arms up and around his neck, her fingertips brushing the light brown hair of his neck. Rising onto her toes to lightly kiss him, she said, "I think you're moving a little too quickly, Chief Lange."

"I am?"

She kissed him again, and he pulled her closer.

"I'll think about it," she said as she pulled away, her face remaining close to his.

His eyes studied her. "You're not one of those women who thinks they should be married before living with someone, are you?"

"Oh, hell, yes, she is," Aunt Judy yelled from where she stood watching them.

"No bedding before the wedding," Sam followed up, still holding Judy's hand.

Jason looked back at Kylie and whispered, "Too late for that."

"I heard that!" Judy shouted.

"Heard what?" Sam asked her.

Jason stood watching Kylie, the question still in his eyes.

"I'll think about it," Kylie smiled flirtatiously up at him.

"Think about what? Moving in or getting married?"

She reached up and gave his lips another soft kiss. "I'll let you know."

Jason gently shook his head as he looked down at her adoringly. "Is there a cupcake recipe I can use to move this along and get an answer out of you?"

"I've got one," Judy shouted again, "and I've been dying to

use it on her."

Kylie dropped her head back as a laugh escaped her lips. "Don't you have somewhere to go, Aunt Judy?"

"All right now, let's leave the kids alone," Sam said, tugging at her hand as she reluctantly trailed after him.

"I can be tricky, too," she called over her shoulder to her niece.

"I may have to enroll her help," Jason said, leaning forward and giving her a light peck before kissing her deeply.

Kylie's hand ran lightly over the stubble on his face as she returned his kiss.

"Mmm, so what do you say?" he asked pulling back. "I know you can't live without me."

Kylie's thumb ran back and forth over the stubble as she looked into his eyes. "I'll let you know, Chief Lange. I'll let you know."

CHAPTER 36

Onadesh stood in the cemetery, looking expectantly at the grave of Little Fawn. "It is time, Little Fawn."

The gentle wind from Lake Michigan blew through the trees in the early evening, but Little Fawn did not appear.

Onadesh looked over his shoulder to the west and the setting sun. "Little Fawn, it is getting late. We must go."

"You found me," she said, suddenly standing beside him and looking down at her grave.

"Yes," came his calm reply. "I told you I would find you, and I did."

She looked up into his hard eyes that softened when meeting hers. "Did it take very long?"

He swallowed hard. "Yes, it took very long."

She nodded in understanding. "The plan did not go as you had hoped."

He reached to feel the softness of her cheek, and his eyes took her in. "No, it did not." His voice caught in his throat. "I am so sorry, Little Fawn. I was the strongest warrior, and I failed you."

Her soft eyes looked up to his with no accusation in them as he continued.

"I looked for you the rest of my life." His hand ran across her cheek before catching in her hair and then following it down. "And now," his hand still holding the ends of her hair, "I cannot stop looking at you."

She smiled up at him. "It is good to see you, too." She wrapped her arms around his neck, and he lifted her to embrace her. "I was so scared, Onadesh. So, so scared," she confided, burying her face in his neck.

"Shh," he gently rocked her, "I am here now. That will never happen again."

She pushed herself inches away to look into his eyes. "It was your arrow that struck me."

His strong jaw tightened. "Yes."

Her eyes, filled with questions, searched his.

"I did not know it was you until I released the arrow," he

told her. "I could not stop it."

"How did the Muscodesh come to our spot? You said I was safe."

"I did not know so many would escape from the village."

"You killed many," she stated flatly.

"Yes."

"You killed me."

"Yes."

Her sad eyes searched his. "You knew I would be there."

"No," he shook his head, "I did not realize we were at our ravine." He eyes lifted as he remembered the day. "I was so tired, Little Fawn. I had not slept for days." He shook his head gently. "There was so much war and killing, it seemed it would never end."

"But it did."

"Yes."

His eyes returned to hers. "I would never harm you, Little Fawn. You know that."

"I know that."

"I have suffered much."

She reached up again and held on tightly to her warrior. "I know. So have I. Promise me, Onadesh. Promise me you will not separate from me again."

"I have been living in hell until now, Little Fawn." His arms held her so close that she could feel her ribs pressing hard against his. "You will never leave my sight."

Tightening her embrace, she giggled happily through her tears. "That is very good."

He spun her around, and they both heard a bark behind them.

"Muckwa, you stayed with me the whole time," Little Fawn told the dog as she left the embrace of Onadesh and ran to the fluffy brown dog. She wrapped her arms around his neck and pressed her face into his thick fur. "You tried to help me, Muckwa. I remember."

The dog let out another bark.

Her embrace tightened. "Thank you, my friend. Thank

you."

"We must go," Onadesh said again as the last rays of sun peeked over the horizon of Lake Michigan.

"We must travel the road of souls?" she asked.

"Yes."

Little Fawn looked down at Muckwa. "Come, Muckwa," she told the dog as she turned and walked to Onadesh.

Hand in hand, the couple walked towards the sunset, the large, brown dog following closely behind them.

"So I'll still be moving into your wigwam when we get there, right?" she teased.

"If they do not have wigwams, I will find a way to build one for you."

"That is very good," Little Fawn said blissfully.

Muckwa let out a yip, and the couple looked ahead.

"Ojig!" Little Fawn shouted gleefully at the sight of her younger brother waving to them ahead.

Onadesh gave her hand a squeeze. "All will be well, Wa-

wash-ay-wesh Koons. All will be well."

EPILOGUE

Ivan Swift tripped miserably along behind his father and brother through the woods of Lower Shore Drive.

"Ivan, keep up," his father called.

"Must the only way I can spend time with you be to follow you and Thorne around as you work?"

His father smiled widely and slowed his pace. Slapping his son's shoulder, he said, "It would be well for you to take over the family business someday." He placed his arm around the young man's shoulders and strode easily over the underbrush next to him.

"The family business is your business, Father. I have my own."

"Ah, yes, the paintings and poetry," his father acknowledged. "But that will not keep a hot meal on your plate."

"Or a woman by your side," Thorne teased from ahead.

Ivan rolled his eyes at his brother who turned and playfully threw a stick that Ivan easily dodged.

"It would be best to learn the family trade, Ivan. Your

brother is the president of the lumber company, is the postmaster, and now surveys this land for development." He turned to look at his youngest son. "You can see why I worry about you."

"I will be fine, Father," Ivan assured.

"Well, it would not hurt to – "

"Father, over here," Thorne called from ahead.

"What is it?" John asked.

Thorne stood with his hands on his hips, staring at the washed-out bluff of the deep inlet. "I – I – " he stumbled, "I think we've found an Indian burial ground."

"Unmarked?" John asked.

Thorne pointed to the remnants of rotted wood. "It looks like there was once a wall here."

"A wall?" John echoed.

The three men stood silently for a moment.

"Why would there be a Native American burial ground in the side of a bluff?" Ivan finally asked.

"It's very odd," John told his youngest son.

"But bones and artifacts have washed out over here," Thorne pointed out.

"Artifacts?" Ivan asked with the first glimmer of interest he'd shown all afternoon.

"Don't touch them," his father cautioned, holding out an arm.

"Why?" Ivan asked, pausing midstride.

"Never disturb a Native American burial site," John warned.

"Oh, come now, Father. Surely you don't believe in curses and ghosts," Ivan held up his hands in an attempt to imitate a menacing creature.

"I've been around long enough to know there are some things you believe in just out of respect," John said.

Ivan dropped his hands and looked soberly at the few bones and bits of pottery that had washed out of the bluff.

"We'll have to build a new wall around it," his father thought out loud. "A wall tall enough to hold back any washout from heavy rains in the future."

"One that will last," his brother agreed.

His father looked over his glasses at both of the boys. "No one is to hear of this, you understand?" Neither son responded. "If folks hear of an Indian burial ground out here, people will get spooked, and the land won't sell." There was still no response. John's focus left the faces of his sons and looked through the woods towards the water. "And this is damn valuable land," his focus returned to his sons, "or at least it will be someday."

Days later, Ivan sat in his folding chair, watching his father and brother build a wall of fieldstone.

"Sure would be nice if you'd help your dear old dad out," John called.

Ivan smiled. "I would love to, Father, but I'm writing something that I must finish."

"Can't you write later?" Thorne asked, moving a heavy stone to rest on the mortar of the rising wall.

"I will lose my thought," Ivan argued, still smiling.

"What do you write this time?" his father asked

absentmindedly as he applied mortar.

"A poem."

"A poem?" Thorne asked in a dismissive tone.

"Some people like them, Thorne," Ivan commented.

"No one I know," Thorne muttered as he turned to search for another stone.

"I believe that," Ivan mumbled to himself under his breath as he wrote.

Hours later, John and Thorne stood next to Ivan's chair admiring the wall.

"Let me see what you've written," John insisted, holding a hand out.

Ivan shrugged. "I don't think it's your cup of tea, but okay."

"Well, read it aloud, Father, so I can hear it as well," Thorne said, leaning to look at the piece of paper.

John read ahead a moment before beginning.

THE TRAIL ROAD
The road that goes to my home
Is my road and my care
And they that take a new road

Have not my hearth to share

I know its long and short faults
And other faults as dear
And variant and hazardous
To fit a man's career

It winds across the mill-creek
And up the Wasson Hill
And after earnest rainfalls
It has a wash to fill

A wall is laid to old walls
To hold the Hurdle Bend
And on the Devil's Elbow
The god of carts defend

But half the good of my road
Is more than half we see
And Indians and old men
And ghosts of men agree

The road that leads the trail way
Is something to remind
And they who travel straight roads
Will leave their roads behind.*1

"Gibberish to me," Thorne dismissed the poem.

John shrugged. "It's a little garbled, but I think I get the gist

of it." He threw the notepad back onto his son's lap and turned to

his other son. "Thorne, I think we're finished here."

Thorne turned to inspect the wall from a distance. "We

should probably throw some dirt around it to hide it." He pointed towards town. "There are no other walls along this whole Lower Shore Drive. Don't want to raise any suspicions."

John nodded. "Good idea." He picked up a shovel and began to follow Thorne back to the wall. "Ivan, grab a shovel."

Ivan let out a deep sigh. "Really?"

"Really. It's getting late, and we want to get out of here." He approached the wall, dug his shovel into the cliff side, and began knocking dirt onto the wall. Ivan followed, picked up a shovel, and half-heartedly began moving dirt against the stone wall.

When the dirt was piled high enough to camouflage the wall, John stuck his shovel into the ground and wiped his brow. Looking at his boys, he reminded, "Remember, no one, not even your mother, is to know about this burial ground or wall. Got it?"

Both boys nodded, Ivan with a mischievous smile on his face.

THE END

*1 – Swift, Ivan. A hand-lettered gift of the author to

Margaret Keydel, early resident of his art colony at Chippewa Cove around the late 1920s. Poem.

A NOTE FROM THE AUTHOR

As a Harbor Springs graduate, I've heard occasional spooky stories about Devil's Elbow since childhood, including the slumber party story that I shared with you in the beginning. Although this is a work of fiction, I worked with the local historians to get as many facts and theories as I could before I began the story.

It's my understanding the entire area from L'Arbre Croche to Cross Village was once heavily populated by the Odawa as well as Manitoulin Island. The story of the Muscodesh is a true part of the Odawa oral history.

If you Google it, one site lists Devil's Elbow as one of the most haunted places in Michigan. Whether it's the story I've woven together or something else, surely there is a reason why so many strange occurrences are reported at this location. Maybe it's just because it's a very dangerous turn in the road, maybe it's because of a death there, or maybe it's because of love lost. Whatever the reason, I hope you enjoyed reading this story as much as I enjoyed writing it. If you enjoyed it and would like to leave a review on

Amazon, it would be much appreciated.

You can find my web site at

www.KDickinson.homestead.com. I discuss dating, love, and

relationships on my blog, found at www.daterella.wordpress.com.

You may contact me at Dickinson.Kristie@gmail.com. Thank you for

reading!

Watch for Book 3 of the Harbor Secret Series in 2017. Other

books by this author:

Nine Days In Greece	The Tunnels
Risking The Nine Days	Devil's Elbow
Before The Nine Days	
Nine Days Ever After	The Back Of His Mind

Made in the USA
Lexington, KY
15 November 2016